East Side Hustler

Leopold Borstinski

ISBN 978 1 913313 17 3   ePub Edition
ISBN 978 1 913313 16 6   Kindle Edition
ISBN 978 1 913313 18 0   Paperback Edition

For more information please visit LeoB.ws

##

JUNE 1919

1

ALEX COHEN TRUDGED along the road until he reached Bay Parkway and McDonald Avenue in Brooklyn, home of the Washington Cemetery. The damp patch in his shoes did nothing to take the piercing chill out of his spine. For a second, he recalled the trenches in France where he'd nearly died more times than he cared to remember.

He shut his eyes and stuffed his hands in his pockets. Ever since he'd returned from the war, a gnawing emptiness had settled in his stomach and refused to go away. The only reason he trudged on was the sure knowledge that many of his comrades had fallen in the Saint-Mihiel attack. That was September 1918 and nine months later, the sound of shells bursting around his ears kept Alex awake at night. And here he was, walking through this garden of stones, hoping to spot one particular slab.

Down the aisles, past decades of death organized in neat rows. He had no clue quite how he would find his objective, but no matter what, he'd have to get to the stone before nightfall.

The disgusted looks flashed at him from various people visiting their loved ones made Alex feel more alone. Like every other cemetery in the world, there was a cold wind blasting across the landscape. He looked down at his clothes and understood why the glances were so judgmental.

A shuffle down another path as leaves flew past him. It was summer and his heart was frozen. Then he stopped and turned to face one stone. Alex read the inscription, a mix of English, Yiddish and Hebrew: Fabian Mustard. The joke name given by a customs officer when he arrived in Ellis Island, like so many other immigrants hoping to find sidewalks paved with gold.

What was going on? How come Fabian was laid to rest here? Alex was confused because the coffin under that tombstone was empty for the simple reason that he was Fabian Mustard and had reverted to his original name when he left for the front.

Some other bums in the Bowery told him his parents bought the plot when they were informed by Uncle Sam that he was dead, but even though he felt like a corpse, he was alive. A tear dripped out of his right eye. The bleakness of seeing his own grave filled him with dread. That gnawing in the pit of his stomach made Alex wretch, and he slumped to the ground, vomit and phlegm mixing on the smooth slab.

When he'd regained his composure, he stood up and slunk out of the cemetery. Before he left, he placed a pebble on Fabian's grave—in the Jewish tradition. In that moment when he hit the dirt, Alex realized he was alone in the world and was a ghost, though still among the living.

After the journey from France, he'd been dumped on the street and told to sort himself out. Three months later and he was no better off than that first day he'd returned to American soil. This shadow-man previously ran a string of gambling pools, extortion rackets and protection across the Bowery and here he was, a nobody with a freshly-dug hole in the ground and a thirst in his throat. Alex trudged back to the Lower East Side and prepared to take his position in the land of the free.

2

EVEN THOUGH ALEX wanted to get back to the Bowery as quickly as possible, the sheer exhaustion he still experienced whenever he put one boot in front of the other prevented him from making much progress. Each time he slumped down to catch his breath or have a nap, the stink of rotting flesh filled his nostrils. When he shut his eyes, he would glimpse someone's head being blown off or the flash-bang of a shell landing.

Nothing would ever be the same again. And when he came back, he couldn't face hanging with his old crowd because they hadn't been there, seen the things he had been forced to see. The taste of the air in his gas mask. The stench of a gangrenous toe. How might a civilian understand the unmentionable acts of survival Alex had endured?

So he kept himself apart from the hustle and the bustle of Bowery life, hunkered down in alleys at night; taking out a begging bowl when the streets filled with normal people. If he was lucky, he'd pick up a few bits; enough for a loaf of bread. The rest he stole.

July segued into August and Alex remained in the gutters around Broome and Columbia. Most days his stomach rumbled but no matter how awful he felt, there was nothing to endure as bad as the war. Those trenches. The mud. That constant foreboding, never knowing if the next moment was your last. Then the whistle would blow and you'd fly over the top and wait to be mown down by enemy fire.

The only thing he was good for was begging. The pitiful looks he received from passersby reflected the physical state he was in. Despite the poverty of the ghetto, there were enough mensches to keep Alex in bread and jam. Sat on the sidewalk with his bowl prominently in front of him, he watched housewives buy food for dinner and saw men pop into cathouses. If they came out thirty minutes later then they'd gone straight upstairs to sample the fleshy wares. If they fell out of the entrance after an hour and staggered down the road, then booze was their vice.

Only once did he imagine he saw his mama and papa but before they came even close, Alex got up and shuffled to another street corner until he was certain they were not heading his way. To bring himself to think beyond the here and now was impossible; the current minute was as far into the future as he could cope with.

ALEX LAY IN an alley with no idea where he was. Somewhere in the Bowery. Curled in a heap, one image repeated in his head: a solitary girl performing a pirouette in her family's living room.

She lived immediately beneath his parent's apartment and her name was Rebecca. She was the most perfect and incredibly beautiful woman Alex ever met. Before basic training, she told him she never wanted to see him again as long as she lived. All he had was the memory of her ankle-length skirt swirling around, lifting until he glimpsed a calf.

Then his thoughts turned to her words, and he wished he could afford a bottle of vodka to drown out the sounds from his head. Instead, he wrapped his arms around his torso as tight as possible and waited for the morning to arrive.

When it did, that skirt continued to spin across the wooden floor and he recalled the gentle touch of her fingertips against his cheek. Having taunted himself to near destruction, Alex got up and shuffled to the main drag to panhandle his way through another day.

Every hour he changed his pitch and tried a different corner. Along the way, he grabbed any scraps of food lying on the floor. In his state, Alex wasn't fussy. He never knew where the next husk of bread would appear, so he paid no never mind if the piece he found was baked in mud or worse. In the trenches, they ate whatever they found to supplement their meager rations. So these morsels almost felt like luxury–only they weren't. He had a sufficient but slender grasp on reality to know how low he had got.

This self awareness fed the grinding ache in his belly and Alex realized he needed to find some way to leave the gutter life, but there was nowhere to go. Then he spotted a flyer fluttering down the street and for no reason at all, he reached out and grabbed it. It was in English but having spent time outside the Jewish shtetl, he now understood what it said.

◆ ◆ ◆

HE PICKED HIMSELF up and shuffled over to the address on the paper. Having shlepped fifteen blocks, Alex found the place quickly. A charity was offering a warm meal and a bed for the night to veterans. At the door, Alex hesitated, but a woman took him by the arm and brought him in. She knew better than to ask a barrage of questions but a quiet calm oozed out of every pore.

Without a word, she led him to a series of tables where a man ladled soup out of an urn and into white bowls.

"There you go, soldier."

"How do you know I'm not just some bum off the street?"

"Are you?"

"No… I once was somebody round here."

"That's good enough for me, Mac."

The guy held a bowl and offered it to Alex. He shrugged and used both hands to carry the steaming broth to the next table where a kindly face added some bread, bobbing on top. For the first time, he checked out the room to see a set of benches in rows for the veterans to use while they ate.

There were huddles of guys talking to each other and a sprinkling of loners. Alex found a bench with nobody sat near it, flopped onto the seat and devoured his meal in record time. The flavors of the soup lingered on his tongue and he considered bargaining for a second portion, but realized his body wasn't equipped for that volume of proper food.

◆ ◆ ◆

INSTEAD ALEX REMAINED seated and cherished the warmth of the room. He had forgotten the simple luxury of being indoors and relished it now. A hobo came over and sat opposite. Alex couldn't decide whether to be annoyed at this imposition on his world or glad of the proximity of another human being. He started with a noncommital grunt, which was mirrored back to him.

The guy concentrated on his soup and enjoyed using his bread to mop up some liquid along the rim of his bowl. Once the meal was over, he raised his gaze to Alex and smiled.

"Tastes good, doesn't it?"

"Yeah."

Despite his best desires, there was nothing else Alex could muster. There was a connection between them—both had lived through hell, but that was their problem. The one thing which bound the two men was so terrible that words failed them. The most they managed was to smile at each other once in a while.

"They serve coffee here too. Want some?"

"Good idea."

Alex followed the regular to the tables and collected a mug of hot brown liquid and the two men returned to their bench.

"Come here often?"

"Couple of times a week. You?"

"First time."

"Thought so. Didn't think I recognized you."

"Been back long?"

"A while, I guess."

"Sorry, don't know why I asked such a stupid question."

"Don't worry about it."

"Just wanted to have a normal conversation, but it was a dumb thing to say."

"I've heard a lot worse."

"The name's Alex."

"Mayson."

"Native New Yorker or never went far from where the boat landed?"

"Born and bred in the island."

"Lived here all the time I can remember."

With that statement, a yawn ripped across Alex's mouth and Mayson grinned.

"They'll shift these benches out of the way soon and bring out the camp beds."

Alex nodded and waited to be enveloped by the warm embrace of unconsciousness.

JULY 1919

3

ALEX VISITED THE soup kitchen once a week, but never more frequently. He knew not to treat the hot meal and warm bed as anything more than a luxury. That way, he didn't get weak.

Bowery streets were the same throughout the neighborhood. Tenement apartments crushed together, families living cheek by jowl. The sidewalks were peppered with stalls and stores offering the usual range of products people need to live a normal life: food, pots, furniture.

Nestling alongside this slice of American civilization was the other face of the area: the bars, cathouses and gambling dens that catered for the many adult vices. This Jewish neighborhood was filled with men and they are the same the world over.

From the safety of his alley, Alex would watch the rats come out in the evening. Some headed for the bars for conversation with friends and an occasional fight with a stranger. Others would nip into a whorehouse but stay for a drink on the first floor afterwards. He recalled the Forsyth Hotel and the Oregon, where his Sarah used to ply her trade. He would sip a beer and wait for her to be free before climbing into her bed and spending the rest of the night in her company. By the end, he didn't even pay for it, although he always left some green as a gift for her.

Her body was a lifetime ago and, despite how hard he tried, he no longer recalled the scent of her neck or the salt of her skin. Those were the memories that had kept him alive in France—and that image of Rebecca spinning round.

The sight of all the offal of humanity degrading and debasing itself every night and most afternoons filled Alex with even more despair. There really was no hope. Not for him, not for anybody. This place was a cesspit and everyone inside it was in a quagmire of depravity. Himself included.

ALEX FORAGED AROUND the back of a bakery one afternoon, hoping to uncover a heap of discarded loaves. Although he only found a crust or two, something about the aroma from the store reminded him of Friday night and his mama's *challah* bread.

In that instant, he crumpled to the ground and cried, tears soaking into the dry earth as soon as they landed. For a moment, he thought about going to the corner of Grande and Suffolk, up onto the fourth floor and wallowing in the joy of his mother's embrace, but he knew he didn't deserve it. Couldn't trust himself around such lovely normal people.

The truth was that despite his medal, Alex was ashamed of what he'd been driven to do in the trenches. What the generals described as bravery, he saw as nothing more than abject cowardice caused by the sheer need to survive. There was no way to bring himself to look Papa square in the eyes.

Somehow he imagined the man would see through him and know the barbarous acts he'd performed to be honored as a hero. What a ridiculous word. An enormous lie. Then Alex recalled the money he'd stashed before his hurried departure to France—as though his brain was trying to drag his attention away from his own thoughts. His own disgust.

All he remembered was shoving five hundred dollars into a sack and carving out a brick from a wall in an alley in the Bowery. If he could've remembered where it was, he'd have grabbed the cash and left New York far behind him. Whenever he concentrated on the image of that hole in the brickwork then his mind's eye would fill up with the whizz and bang of shells landing around him. He cowered waiting for the nonexistent barrage to stop.

Alex knew he could not continue living this way. He considered hitching a ride on a freight train out of town, but the thoughts in his skull would follow him wherever he traveled. He had to do something else, and he'd figured out exactly what that was.

4

ALEX SHUFFLED OUT of his alley and passed down the sidewalk, stealing some apples as he went. They crunched loudly in his head and he almost choked with the amount of juice in his mouth. He continued on his way, grabbing items off stalls as he walked. He even popped into a store or two, but found beady eyes staring at him, making it impossible for him to rob from the glaring owners.

In the end, his pockets were full, and he squatted at the corner of Bayard and Bowery. Alex shoveled some bread into his mouth and chewed the pieces until there were only crumbs left on his fingers. Then he devoured his last apple and threw the core into the gutter. Still savoring the taste, he leaned back against a wall and soaked in the scene surrounding him.

There were the usual scurrying housewives and men weaving around the sidewalks. Some guys drank from dawn to dusk—and beyond. In France, he'd gulped down whiskey when he had the chance, but there was never enough to remove the memories in his head—just sufficient to help him fall asleep. And the same images would haunt him again when he awoke.

Alex pulled out the knife from his tattered coat pocket. He had found the garment on the corpse of a hobo two weeks before. When he first wore it, the garment stank of death but he'd got used to the stench and stopped noticing by the second morning.

With the blade in one hand, he pulled back his sleeve to reach his wrist. He knew he'd never be able to slice his throat open but his wrist…

Alex gripped the handle tightly and moved the sharp metal onto his skin. Then he inhaled deeply, knowing the next moment would be decisive. Just as he was about to cut deep into his flesh, a hand came from nowhere and prized the knife out of his grasp.

He growled and turned his head up to see this interloper. The face scowling down at him was familiar but he couldn't quite place it. The man was from a time before France. When the trenches were just a phrase uttered by a sergeant at boot camp.

The fella continued to grimace at him as Alex stared back. Schmendrik. What was his problem and why did he think Alex's life was any of his business?

"Dear boy, we thought you were dead."

The Yiddish sentence floated into his ears and the voice almost sounded concerned. He continued to sit with his blank expression. Gar nichts.

"How long have you been back?"

Alex focused hard on the mouth, nose and eyes of the speaker until the face became familiar.

"Waxey?"

The gang boss smiled and held out his hand. Alex took it and stood up.

"Let's get you cleaned up. I'm guessing you haven't eaten in a while and I have to tell you, buddy, you stink. *Verstinkener schlemiel.*"

WAXEY GORDON LED Alex into his clubhouse on the corner of the street. The place had been decorated since the last time he'd been inside and a bright red-and-white sign adorned the frontage. The man didn't feel the need to hide his whereabouts; he was king of the heap.

Alex followed his former boss up to the second floor and flopped into the old meeting room. A couch had been added to the roster of shabby furniture but nothing else had changed. Even the stale smell of sweat and coffee still lingered in the air.

A steaming mug appeared in front of him and Alex placed a hand either side as though to warm up, but his body wasn't cold. Just his aching head. He looked up and found he was alone so he remained sat at the table and enjoyed the sensation of being inside a building. The walls, floor and ceiling offered a comfort—their very solidity giving him some of the security and certainty he craved.

Ira Moskowitz entered the room and approached him.

"Waxey said it was you, but I couldn't believe my ears. How are you doing? Don't answer that. I can see exactly. We need to get you some new clothes and introduce you to the dark art of a bath. No offense, friend."

A light squeeze of the shoulder was all Alex could cope with before he edged his torso away from Waxey's right-hand man. Ira wasn't offended and relaxed on the couch, spreading himself out and enjoying a moment's tranquility in an otherwise hectic day.

Alex barely recognized the man, but despite his overall caution built up from months living on the street, he felt no ill will toward the guy who seemed harmless enough. Waxey returned to explain that he'd made a few calls and found a place for him to go. There was an unnecessary smile on Waxey's face but Alex was in no mood for any games the fella was playing.

Fifteen minutes later, Alex stood at the entrance of the Oregon Hotel. The bar stretched along one wall opposite a smattering of tables. Alex dug his hands deep in his coat pocket and tensed his arm muscles as he recognized the interior and remembered who lived here.

As if on cue, Sarah trotted down the stairs and a smile ripped across her face as she caught sight of him. She bundled him in her arms and took him upstairs for a long soak in a bath and the chance to lie on her bed.

If she'd been planning anything more for their reunion, she would have been bitterly disappointed. As soon as Alex's head hit the feathery down of the pillow, he fell fast asleep.

◆ ◆ ◆

SMOKE. MUD. BLOOD. Alex popped his eyes above the rim of his foxhole long enough to see the flames around the sniper's rifle in the distance. Maybe sixty or eighty feet away. An incredibly loud whizzing sound made him cover one ear with his left hand; his right clutched his weapon and nothing was going to separate him from that. His ears still ringing, he leaped out of the slush pit with a single aim to reach the sniper before the German spotted him and fired. Bobby was screaming in agony somewhere in the no-man's land ahead.

ALEX WOKE TO find himself naked and under layers of blankets. He covered his face with the sheets and inhaled, taking in Sarah's aroma and the smells of her bedroom. Sex mixed with sorcery. A chair creaked, and he saw her sit up, eyes barely open. She must have given up her bed.

Strange, because they'd shared this bed for months before he went to war—not that he had the strength or any inclination to do anything more than lie in the same room as Sarah at the moment.

"Do you fancy a bite to eat, Fabian?"

"Don't use Fabian: he died in France. My name is Alex Cohen."

"Seems peculiar to change what I call you."

"Believe me when I tell you that fella is dead. I've visited his grave so it must be true."

Sarah rolled her eyes and looked around for a smoke.

"Your parents are sentimental types."

She offered a cigarette and he accepted it. Since his return to America, the only cigarettes Alex had found were discarded butts. The luxury of his own tobacco overwhelmed him and salty water dribbled out of his eyes, splashing onto the white sheets. Sarah moved on the bed and wrapped her arms around him.

Alex hugged her and cried for what felt like a lifetime, but eventually his tears dried up and he was able to let go.

"Some lokshen soup?"

"And a coffee if there's any going spare."

"I'm sure we can stretch to a hot drink. Do you want anything stronger?"

He shook his head.

"That'd just knock me out. I've not had much to eat these last few weeks. Not since I returned…"

"…from the fighting?"

"From France."

Sarah nodded and left to get the food, leaving Alex sat up in bed with a half-view out of the window. He didn't want to leave his sanctuary and slid back down under the covers. When she returned with a tray, Sarah found him snoring away but the smell of the soup roused him from slumber.

She spooned the hot liquid into his mouth and Alex allowed her, even though he was more than capable of feeding himself. This was the first time he'd been able to trust the world long enough to let his guard down and subsume himself into somebody else's protection.

And it was his Sarah. When they'd seen each other last, he'd kissed her on the lips and said goodbye as though that day was like any other. But it was the morning he shipped out of New York after volunteering to fight the Hun.

He'd forgotten his reasons for going and he doubted if they'd made much sense even then. No matter how much training you receive, nothing prepares you for trench warfare.

Then he allowed his mind to wander and he remembered the times he and Sarah had spent in that bed. The things they'd got up to and the conversations which had taken place. Hopes and dreams laid bare. An honesty between them that he'd torn apart when he scurried away to France without telling her either that he was going or what was his destination.

SEPTEMBER 1919

5

OVER THE NEXT two months, Alex spent his time with Sarah and for the first three weeks he didn't leave her bedchamber. His strength returned once his body got used to eating ordinary food again and the atrocious images flying across his head seemed to wane. At least for now. This gave him an opportunity to rebuild bridges with his former lover.

"You never explained why you didn't tell me you were going off to fight."

"I couldn't find the words and was afraid of how you'd react."

"What did you imagine I would do?"

"Not really sure anymore. Then, you were my bedrock, my anchor, and if you had turned your back on me, then I can't imagine what I'd have done."

Alex stared out of the window, not daring to make eye contact. Sarah put her hand on his.

"You weren't listening to me in that case. I said I would change my life around to live with you. To be your wife."

He darted a glance in her direction and nodded.

"Yeah, but I was stupid enough not to hear your words. All the trouble with Sammy and what was going on with Rebecca…"

"Complicated, but it doesn't have to be like that. When you recover, you'll leave this room and maybe return to see me. The important thing for me is that you understand one message: I would drop my current life in an instant if you said you would commit to me."

"How would we get by?"

"We'd earn like everybody does—only there'd be nobody else either of us would sleep with. This would be our bed—in every sense."

Alex sandwiched Sarah's hand in his palms and squeezed gently.

"I'm not disregarding what you've said, but I can't deal with that right now. Not because I'm not interested in you—far from it—but because I'm finding it hard to focus on the future; I have spent so much time only concentrating on where the next meal will come from. Long-term planning is thinking about tomorrow, for me, and anything bigger than that has to be put on ice."

SARAH SIGHED, NODDED and withdrew her hand. Alex wondered if he'd said too much. He was amazed she wanted to spend her time with him and hadn't considered the practicalities: if she was with him all day and all night then how was she paying for the room and board?

A moment's reflection by Alex and he would have realized that Waxey was paying the bills. Who else would be that generous or have deep enough pockets? No one that Alex knew. Instead, he kept his existence wrapped inside a tiny ball comprising his next meal, staying warm and enjoying Sarah's company.

"This isn't where I ever imagined we'd be."

"What do you mean, Alex? I'd got used to having you around before you skipped town. I took ages to fill the Fabian-sized gap in my life."

"How d'you do that? With someone?"

"No need to be like that. You left me—remember that before you try to take any high moral ground."

"Says the *nafka* to the former gangster."

"And less of the whore, if you don't mind. You sound like the rest of them, judging me."

"Oh no, Sarah. I'm not being snarky."

"You sure sounded like it. You have no idea what I go through every moment I walk along the sidewalk."

But he did. Not before France, but Alex had spent enough time on the streets to appreciate the dangers the nafkas put themselves through as they went past ordinary men with lustful ideas.

"Sarah, did Waxey tell you what I've been through since I got back from the front?"

"This isn't about you. I'm the one you just insulted."

He was silent for a spell, mulling over what she'd said and how arrogant his response had been to her. He hadn't meant to be like that, but his paranoia about what she had done while he was overseas had overtaken him.

"Look, I'm sorry. It hurts me that you survived okay without me and my tongue lashed out just then. Nothing more than that."

Sarah uncrossed her arms and there was a silence between them for a minute.

"LISTEN TO ME, Sarah. This is important. I appreciate all you've done for me these past couple of months and I've been remembering our time together before…"

Alex's voice trailed off as his mind wandered to France, but quickly he snapped to the present.

"We were good together, weren't we?"

Her nod confirmed his belief.

"And I was wrong to push you away. Back then and now, although since Waxey found me, I've not been my full self."

"When you first were brought into this room, you were like a small child. So frail, so needy. You couldn't feed yourself, you were so weak."

"I'm stronger and ready to face the world again, but not alone. I want you with me."

Sarah leaned over to kiss him firmly on the lips and Alex responded by gingerly placing his palms on her cheeks to engulf her head in his hands. She made him happy—he realized that now—and he didn't want them to be apart.

He stood up and encouraged her to follow him until they reached the side of the bed. Then he removed her clothes, and they clambered under the sheets.

Later when they were sharing a cigarette, Alex stared at her body and wondered what would happen now.

"I've big dreams, Sarah, and this time I want you to be a part of them."

"You've heard my answer too many times before."

"I'm listening this time. You have to trust me when I tell you I choose to be with you. And we are going places. I will never be in the position I've just recovered from. Not again so long as I live and that's a stone-cold promise. I shall go back to work for Waxey until I'm so filthy rich that money is never a problem again. I will never have to panhandle for food or shelter. And neither will you. That is my commitment to you today. Right now we are surrounded by the scum of the Bowery, but one day we'll live the high life in the best part of the Lower East Side."

Sarah sat up, smiled and kissed him on the forehead. She'd spent enough time in bed with men to know when they were lying to her and deep in her heart she knew that Alex was telling the truth.

"One day, you and I will be on top of the world."

"You'd better get some sleep, Slugger."

"That's not my name anymore. He died a long time ago in a foreign field."

"Sure thing, honey."

They rolled over and soon snored loud enough to wake the dead.

6

THE NEXT DAY, Alex hopped out of bed, kissed Sarah on the forehead and made his way out of the Oregon. He blinked in the early morning light and stormed off to the corner of Bayard and Bowery. A nod to the guard on the door and up the stairs to find Waxey and Ira.

He discovered them eating breakfast over a newspaper in their favorite room. His boss beckoned him to join them and he poured himself a coffee and offered the two men a refill, but both declined. Alex waited as long as he could but the fellas were too engrossed in their reading matter to bother to acknowledge him any further. A polite cough achieved nothing.

"I've got a question to ask you."

"Dear boy, I'm all ears."

Waxey winked at Ira over his lowered paper and pretended to lean toward Alex to hear him better.

"I have known you two ever since I came to this country some five years ago."

"And every day has been a pleasure."

Ira smirked at Waxey's interruption but said nothing.

"Thanks, Waxey, but we both know that isn't entirely the case… Anyway, I was a good earner for you for quite a while but I am very aware I haven't paid my way since you helped me back on my feet."

"We're not asking for payback, Alex. We live together, we fight together..."

"...and I nearly died alone."

A silence descended as the three mulled over the implications of Alex's words. He'd been part of a tight crew and had run his men with an iron hand and a fair tone to his voice. That said, each knew he had run away from the Bowery and Waxey's gang.

He might have told Waxey what he was planning to do, but he most definitely hadn't asked permission. There was something in Waxey's expression which echoed those thoughts. No one had implied it but everybody was thinking it.

"I walked out of this room like a *schnorrer*. I was running away from my problems and didn't know which way to turn."

"The army wouldn't have been my first port in a storm."

"The boy left the thighs of one of our best nafkas to fight strangers in a far-off land."

"I thought I was going to save the Jews who hadn't made it to America. The ones who were still facing the pogroms."

"And did you?"

"Nope."

"Did you see any Jews when you were over there?"

"Only one."

"Oh? What was he like?"

"Devastatingly handsome and real funny, told brilliant stories, but no luck with any of the local ladies until he learned some American and a few French phrases."

"Where d'you see him, this raconteur?"

"In the shaving mirror every morning."

They laughed, and the chuckles carried on coming out of Alex's mouth long after the joke wasn't funny anymore. The whole point of him going was to follow Monk Eastman's advice and free the Jews who couldn't escape. Eventually the laughing subsided.

"Waxey, you were right. Monk was a washed-up has-been by the time I spoke with him. What the hell was I thinking?"

"Don't be overly hard on yourself; you were young and naïve. Thought you could rule the world and had all the answers."

"You're too kind, Ira. I was dumb and arrogant—a dangerous combination."

"Before you left, you took care of business. Don't be too harsh on yourself—leave that to others."

"Thank you. How are what remains of my crew?"

"Surviving, but safe and well."

Alex recalled the last time he'd seen Abraham and Paulie as they chased him onto the platform and his locomotive stole out of the station to take him to basic training.

"Still want to kill me?"

He savored a long mouthful of coffee just in case it was his last. Waxey must have issued the order, and the guys were merely doing what they'd been instructed. Would the tsuris with Sammy ever go away?

"The boys bear you no ill will, you can be sure of that."

"And how about you, Waxey?"

"I told you, Alex, that if I ever found out that you murdered Sammy then I would have you killed, but you are alive, standing in front of me so there is no way that I ordered a hit on you."

"So why were they chasing me? They certainly intended to do me harm."

"Perhaps they had their own agenda to follow. Maybe they felt betrayed by your sudden unannounced departure…"

"…or they didn't believe your story about Sammy getting set upon by the Yake Brady gang and vanishing in a puff. We never found his body."

Alex eyed Ira's expression to discern why he was mentioning all this detail like it was yesterday. Like he wanted Alex to know he was the one who ordered the hit and hadn't forgotten. Alex swallowed and moistened his lips with his tongue.

"What's done is done, though. Right, Ira?"

"So they say, Alex."

Alex glanced between the two men, unsure how much they were playing him. Sarah had explained to him that Waxey had gone up in the world and now had his fingers in most pies in the Lower East Side. Along the way, he'd picked up some mighty powerful—and dangerous—friends.

"Are we good, Waxey?"

"As I see it, Alex, when Sammy met his maker, he left this world with nothing of any material value. When you arrived at my front step, you possessed nothing too. You balance each other out and there is no more to say on the matter."

"Ira?"

"What Waxey says is fine by me. Sammy's dead and you're alive. And a war hero too."

"I wouldn't go that far."

"Sarah says the *goyim* gave you a medal."

Alex stared at the ground and tapped a boot. He recalled scrabbling up a mound with sniper fire all around. For that they handed out medals.

"You've embarrassed the boy, Ira. Let's talk of happier matters. Alex, when will you be well enough to run your own crew?"

THEY SAT AROUND a solitary table, a beer in front of every man. Alex surveyed the scene and tried to judge how things were going. Abraham seemed the most happy to see him and Paulie appeared to sulk almost before Alex entered the joint. Then there were two new guys.

Ezra Kohut had lived in the tenements of the Bowery all his life. He blended into the bar, looking like any other customer who ever ordered a beer. His family had come over at the end of the last century and Ezra had been born within a spit of their table.

Massimiliano Sciarra, Massimo for short, was Italian and had joined up with Waxey at the suggestion of Charlie Lucky around the time of the trouble with the Yake Brady gang. Having proved himself as an excellent fighter, Waxey asked Charlie if the fella could stay on the team and Charlie agreed.

Alex sipped his brew and allowed the other fellas to take control of the conversation. Besides, he wasn't feeling supremely confident inside himself. The guys talked about the neighborhood and their most recent sexual conquests. There was no mention of anything that happened more than two weeks ago and they referred to Alex only twice in the first thirty minutes. He reckoned this was his punishment from Abraham and Paulie, while Massimo and Ezra had no idea of the game being played.

The four men gave Alex the strong impression that they ruled their territory with an iron fist—Abraham and Paulie had learned well from him. Waxey had explained how their previous gang leader had met with an unfortunate accident—a knife plunged deep into the small of his back. Unlucky for him but great news for Alex because he could work with some fellas from before the war even if they weren't too happy to see him.

"Sure is good to see you guys again."

Grunts for replies and sipping of beer.

"When I left in a hurry, we didn't get a chance to say goodbye properly."

"That's because you ran away."

"I needed to leave, Abraham. And you chased after me. Remember?"

"Do you think either of us would forget that morning?"

"No, Paulie, but there's been a lot of time between then and now."

All five stared into their glasses but Alex was the first to look up and glance around.

"I knew that if I told you guys what I was planning on doing..."

"Fight for the goyim?"

"Fight to free the Jews who hadn't made it over here."

"Now you sound like Moses."

"I took advice from Monk Eastman."

"You knew him?"

"We only met twice but he made a big impression on me."

Eastman was a legend. An ox of a man who ruled the Lower East Side at the turn of the century but couldn't reinvent himself for the modern world. Alex understood that now.

"I made a mistake. More than one, to be honest. I shouldn't have just walked away. I was wrong and I apologize to you."

"Takes a big man to admit when he's wrong."

Paulie stood up and shook Alex's hand. Abraham shrugged and repeated the gesture. The other two downed their beers because Alex wasn't really speaking to them, anyway.

"Let me get another round. You guys look thirsty."

"I'll buy you a beer with a whiskey chaser."

"Thanks, Abraham."

For the first time since he'd sat at the table, Alex felt accepted—if only by one of the squad. Paulie's eyes remained transfixed on him but he didn't utter a single word for another five minutes. Then he sprang up, teetered gently because of the alcoholic effect of the brew and slurred an announcement.

"To the past and our future! To Sammy and Alex."

Two years ago and the shrewish Italian wouldn't have had the confidence or the audacity to speak up that way. All the while, his eyes pierced through Alex like a sniper's bullet.

He stared back at Paulie and raised his glass before taking a swig of beer that caused him to wipe away a white foam mustache with his sleeve.

"Brave and true words, my friend."

The rest of the group went silent as soon as Paulie fell back onto his chair. Alex continued maintaining a calm voice which possessed only a whisper of malice.

"Sammy is dead, for sure, and I was one of the last people to see him alive. I have witnessed many deaths in my short time on this earth. Young lives lost in battle abroad and at home. The Yake Brady war might only have lasted a week or two but it was brutal and blood was shed on both sides—theirs more than ours. Sammy is gone and Waxey has made his peace with this. If any of you cannot do the same, then you should speak here and now."

Alex took a sip from his beer and eyeballed each of the fellas, leaving Paulie until last. No one raised any objections and their eyes attempted to drown in their glasses.

"That settles the matter then. I loved Sammy and I am very sorry he's gone but tears won't bring back the dead. There were rumors I killed him but anyone who knew me then would attest to how I dealt with guys: a blade across the throat or a fist into your face. From what I understand, they never found Sammy's body, and that really isn't my style."

Paulie ground his molars but said zip. Whatever he thought happened back then, he could do nothing about it today. Alex was here and Sammy was not. *Shoyn.*

"To the future, Alex. I'm glad you are here and let's look forward to a prosperous tomorrow."

A clink of glasses all round and the men settled in for an evening's drinking. When the fellas wanted to move upstairs and sample the fleshy delights on offer at the bar, Alex bid them well and returned to the warmth and comfort of Sarah's bed.

DECEMBER 1919

7

LAST NIGHT'S BAR became today's office as Alex had yet to earn himself a slot in Waxey's headquarters, let alone winning back his old job as a union convener. To achieve that, he'd need to deliver something special, and the opportunity came knocking that morning.

The Mercury Hotel's drinking area led straight from the street. Any hapless individual who thought they wanted to stay the night would check in with the barman. Most of the residents were regulars who flouted the no-fraternization rule hourly. *Nafkas* popped downstairs with the sole purpose of picking up their next john.

Alex and his crew sat near to the rear of the establishment and he made sure he had his back to the wall. After he'd downed his first coffee of the day, a boy shuffled in and headed for Abraham. The kid whispered in his ear, Abraham nodded, smiled and gave the boy a nickel for his trouble.

"Something's up at the docks, according to my *boychik*."

"Worth standing up for?"

"There's gelt to be made if we play it right."

"Then stop sitting on your *tuches* and let's get over there."

THE FIVE MEN strode east from Columbia and Broome until they reached Pier 47 and then pushed north to Pier 50 and Rivington

Street. A large warehouse faced the East River with gates the height of four people—at first glance. When they looked again, they noticed there was a normal door embedded in the right-hand portcullis. The words above the wrought-iron fence were rusted but told them everything they needed to know: Clinemann Clothing.

Rat-a-tat and they walked straight in. There was a dingy entranceway with an office on the left side, seats on the right and a wall up ahead. They could feel the sound of factory machinery in their rib cages. A constant judder like an impending earthquake. Alex entered the room without knocking and instructed his men to wait.

"Where is Mr. Clinemann?"

"Do you have an appointment?"

The secretary behind the desk was unimpressed by Alex's brusque manner but he continued, anyway.

"My name is Alex Cohen and Clinemann needs to speak with me."

"*Mister* Clinemann decides who he sees and not the other way around."

He stood still and played with the change in his pocket, making sure the woman heard the jangling over the hum of the factory. Then he waited some more.

"I asked where he is and I recommend you answer my question. You wouldn't want anything unfortunate to befall you."

Alex's gaze wandered over to one wall which comprised glass windows all along and a curtain to hide the workers busy at their toil. Then he returned his gaze to Ravid Gardner. Her cheeks reddened to a pink as her eyes followed the trajectory indicated by Alex's look. Was he going to throw her through the window? Very unlikely. Did she know that? Not at all.

There were two doors in the wall behind Ravid, one either side of her desk. She leaned her head to one side and glanced in one direction long enough for Alex to understand. He nodded, breezed past her and entered the inner chamber to see an average man in a black suit with a narrow mustache sitting behind a large oak desk.

"I'm so sorry, Mr. Clinemann, he barged his way through."

Alex let Ravid's lie hang in the air because it stopped Clinemann concentrating on more important matters until Alex cleared his throat to get Clinemann's attention.

ALEX CLOSED THE door on Ravid's protestations and waited to discover how this pinhead would react. Clinemann leaned back in his chair, fingertips pressed together and stared at Alex. He separated his fingers long enough to beckon Alex to sit down but remained silent.

"Thank you for taking the time out of your busy schedule to see me."

"You have forced yourself into my office without permission, but my guess is that you didn't visit my premises alone."

"Correct."

"And this is why I am not making a fuss. I imagine we have business to attend and you are not a fellow to take 'no' for an answer."

"Right, again. As you are showing remarkably clear insight, tell me why I am here, invading your day and disgruntling your employees?"

"I have my suspicions, but in matters of business, I do not play games. Explain why you are here and we can proceed further in our discussions."

Now it was Alex's turn to lean back in his chair to leave Clinemann hanging for a response. To stretch out time Alex lit a cigarette and cupped the lit end in his palm, a habit he'd gained in the trenches.

"You owe us money and we are here to collect."

"Forgive me, Mister…"

"Cohen."

"…but I don't hand my money over to any old hoodlum who comes bustling along. Panhandlers can take a walk."

A drag on his cigarette and, as Alex exhaled, a plume of smoke erupted from his month, mixing with his words.

"Mr. Gordon would not be impressed if he learned you were welching on a deal."

The color drained from Clinemann's cheeks. For all his bravura, he'd no idea what Alex was doing until he heard the name of the boss of the Lower East Side.

"I meant no disrespect."

"Apology accepted. I have been overseas until recently and you probably didn't recognize me."

"Sorry, but your name is not familiar to me."

"I used to be known as Fabian Mustard."

Although Alex hadn't thought it possible, Clinemann's complexion went a paler shade of white. Alex remained silent as he stubbed out his cigarette.

"So now we've introduced ourselves, let's get down to business. Perhaps your secretary can bring us a coffee to lubricate the conversation?"

"Of course."

"My men would appreciate something too."

Clinemann rang a bell and Ravid scurried in to do her master's bidding.

"I KNEW SOMEONE would visit me eventually."

"And you chose not to preempt this inevitable situation by seeking out Mr. Gordon?"

"To be honest, Mr. Cohen, I didn't see the point. From what I've gathered, if you don't pay up, the visit occurs no matter who you speak to beforehand."

The guy had a point, but nothing would shift Alex from his perch on top of the high moral ground. He'd lived through this routine too many times before.

"You don't seem to understand the difficult position you've put yourself in."

Clinemann shrugged, as though he knew what was coming next and had resigned himself to the whole shebang. Alex might not have hustled anybody for protection money for a year or two, but he didn't think he'd seen anyone behave this way before.

"How much gelt do you have on the premises?"

"Chump change. If I had what I owed, then I wouldn't put myself in this situation. Don't misunderstand me. This is a problem I don't want to have, but here we are."

"Where's the money? I understood your business is doing swell."

"Don't believe everything people say. Listen to the machines."

Alex strained his ears and discerned only the clatter of metal on metal.

"What am I supposed to notice?"

"The sound of non-union labor operating slowly. At the rate these guys take, I'll be lucky to get any garments packed and out by the end of the week."

"Scabs. What's the trouble with the unions?"

"Pay and conditions; the usual. Seems we aren't treating them fairly."

"Are you?"

Clinemann shrugged with the same level of detachment as his talk of money earlier. Could he really be playing things this cool and bluffing Alex?

"So you have two problems. My money and your workers. Resolve the second and the former appears."

"That's the long and the short of it."

BACK AT THE Mercury, Alex sipped a drink and considered his options while the other fellas went about their morning collections. Capital and labor were always at odds with each other, but he had never been on either side. To him, there was no right or wrong in this battle. The average working Joe was a *schnook* in his eyes and the bosses were no better.

Naturally, his ambivalence was masked to both sides by his apparent desire to help them. This strategy had worked over and over again in the past, but he was less certain it would succeed this time. To begin with, the modern world included a Russia where a people's revolution had taken place and unions knew they had strength behind them.

Abraham arrived first and grabbed a beer from Uriel Menahem at the bar. He slumped onto his seat and chugged back half his brew in one swallow.

"Thirsty?"

Abraham smiled and nodded.

"How do you think we should convince the union to play ball with Clinemann?"

"Find the local convener and grab them by the balls until they see sense. People overthink these problems, but we live in simple times and deal with simple folk. Arrange an appointment, will you?"

8

THE LOCAL CHAPTER of the Machinists and Sewers Union had its own offices in a building close to the Clinemann warehouse, two blocks north, because the docks always offered the cheapest accommodation due to the stench of the East River.

Guys played cards, sipped drinks and talked to each other. An untrained eye could be forgiven for believing that Alex had stumbled into an ordinary bar. But he was here to see one particular person and no other. Up to the barman and a simple question.

"Marvyn Beck?"

A solitary finger pointed at an individual in the far corner seated by himself. Ten seconds later and Alex sat opposite him, although Marvyn refused to acknowledge his presence. Alex waited as long as he could to give the guy a chance to behave like a man but Marvyn chose not to.

"I believe you've been expecting me. My people got in contact yesterday."

"Yes, but that doesn't mean I must be happy about it, given your... provenance."

"I come in peace and I'm hoping we'll be able to talk matters through to everyone's advantage—including your members."

"What has Clinemann sent you over to say that he couldn't tell me directly?"

"Marvyn, I represent a separate set of interests to your boss. Your concerns and mine are perfectly aligned. The only difference is that you care about the welfare of your members and I don't. They can live or die and I will sleep equally soundly tonight."

The guy looked straight at Alex all this while and had shrugged off his sullen disposition.

"What does Gordon want? And how much is it going to cost us?"

"No need to drag Waxey into this. You and I are talking; that is who you are dealing with. You know who I represent and have done your research on me. Congratulations. If my reputation precedes me, we can conduct ourselves in a constructive manner and get everything resolved before lunch. I assume the food here is decent?"

"Good enough for a working man."

"That's more than a recommendation for me."

Alex ordered a coffee and returned to the table.

"What do you want from Clinemann?"

"More pay. Better conditions."

"And in exchange for the moon, you'll go back to work?"

"Of course. Everybody wants to earn a crust. We strike because we have no other option. We demanded paid sick leave for six months, but he didn't budge, even though people's lives were put in danger every day. Women are losing limbs, and their children starve to death because he won't spend the money to service and repair the machinery. The *gonif.*"

"ARE YOU TELLING me this whole mess could be sorted out by getting a maintenance crew out to the factory?"

"If only it was that simple, Alex. The problem isn't just about the repairs. Clinemann has no respect for any of us. We're cogs in his machine, not people with families, hopes and dreams."

"What does that mean? You're there to work, not to have him finance your life."

"He acts like he doesn't trust us. If anything goes wrong, he blames the workers first before finding out the real cause, which is usually his managers. Pay peanuts and you get monkeys."

"I gotta tell you, I knew this was coming. When all's said and done, every union rep I've met bleats on about conditions, but what they always really want to talk about is money. No disrespect intended, Marvyn."

"None taken. And I want to improve the welfare of my members. That's why the union exists."

Alex had heard it all before, but beneath every union official was a grifter seeking fresh ways to make a turn. Some were brazen and asked for a slice of the action whereas others played around, not wanting to be seen to be conniving, money-grabbing charlatans. Marvyn fell into the latter camp.

"How can I help? A crew could fix the machinery in the morning; say the word and I will organize it. If there's anything else I can do, let me know. I want the strike to be over and your workers to be back, happy and churning out product."

"Schmatta to be precise."

"Whatever. What do you need to return to work? Tell me and I shall make it happen."

Marvyn sat back in his chair, thought for a minute, chugged some of his drink and leaned forward with both elbows on the table. Alex mirrored the move to add to the conspiratorial atmosphere.

"Fifty cents an hour for my people and fifty dollars a month for me and each of the reps at the factory. And the repair crew."

"Anything else?"

"No, that's all. Can you deliver that for me, Alex?"

"That is well within my grasp. Let's finish our conversation as we walk you home."

Marvyn nodded, and they sauntered out after Alex paid the bar bill.

THEY STOPPED WHEN they arrived at Marvyn's tenement and almost without thinking, he invited Alex inside. By the time they reached the fifth floor Alex was out of breath. He might be on the mend but he had not yet fully recovered. He rested, leaning on a wall, as Marvyn brought him a glass of water.

"Do you think I could sit down for a short while?"

Marvyn led him inside and he slumped onto a dining room chair. While he regained his composure, Alex used the time to look around. The place was the usual mix of cheap furniture and screaming children, who were old enough to sew but still too young to keep quiet in the evening when adults were talking.

Near the kitchen door stood his wife, one baby clasped to her hip, peering round the doorway at the stranger in her home. He smiled and walked over to make a fuss of the little 'un in her arms.

"You haven't introduced us, Marvyn. I'm Alex—and you are…?"

"…Rachel, and this is Samuel."

Without a word, Alex reached his arms out and Rachel placed Samuel in his care. Alex bounced the boy up and down until he gurgled playfully. Within two minutes he'd put the babe down. Samuel was too young to scuttle off by himself and remained on the floorboards where Alex had rested him.

He shoved his hands in his pants pockets and looked embarrassed to be surrounded by such an adorable family. An instant later, he pulled out a shiv, grabbed Rachel by the wrist and planted an arm around her torso. The blade stood ready, an inch away from her throat.

"Now I have your attention, Marvyn, it's time for you to hear my terms."

"YOU MISUNDERSTOOD HOW this all works. As you can see, I hold your family's life in my hands and you thought you should shake me down for fifty bucks a month."

Marvyn's eyes darted from Alex to Rachel and back again. He gulped hard but remained silent.

"So this is what we will do. You send everyone to return to work tomorrow. As a sign of appreciation I will not kill your wife or your children."

Marvyn swallowed again and licked his lips while Rachel carried on whimpering. Alex stared straight at Marvyn.

"If you do this for me, I shall ensure that Clinemann gets the machines repaired and I will look to getting your members a better rate of pay. I am sure he will see reason. But that is all that will happen. Your workers' lives will be improved because you have told me that is important to you."

To emphasize his point, Alex pushed his blade close to Rachel's throat, all the while staring at Marvyn.

"The only outstanding matter is that your family is clearly not safe; look at what you have allowed to happen here."

A tear rolled out of Marvyn's eye and he rubbed it away.

"You must get some insurance to protect yourself."

"Protection?"

"Yes, you will need to pay me to ensure your family stays safe. How you secure the fee is up to you. Pay it from your own pocket or raise your members' dues. I don't care. If you don't settle with me, harm will inevitably befall your kin. Give me my money and they live to a ripe old age. The choice is yours."

Marvyn nodded consent and Alex relaxed his grip on Rachel who felt as though she was about to crumple onto the floor. The knife remained by her throat because Alex couldn't be certain Marvyn wouldn't try something stupid. The pathetic lump of humanity before him showed no signs of being dangerous, but Alex knew how quickly calm situations can turn into bloody mayhem—in France or in the Lower East Side.

Alex lowered his knife hand and kept his other on Rachel in case of need.

"Stay where you are and I shall let go of her. Do you understand?"

A nod from Marvyn and yet another whimper from his wife. All the time, the kids were playing or simply gurgling on the floor as though everything was completely normal. They ignored the adult world this evening as they did any other night.

Twenty seconds later and Rachel grabbed their youngest in her arms and hustled the children into the bedroom where they remained, door shut.

"I shall leave you to decide what is an appropriate amount to pay each month to keep your family from harm. Naturally, if the sum ever falls short of what is needed…"

"…then you'll hurt them."

"You understand completely. Make the first instalment tomorrow morning. You'll find me at the Mercury. You can provide the second payment six weeks later and monthly thereafter without fail."

Alex called goodbye to Rachel, but all he achieved was to make her cry again. He shrugged and left the Beck apartment.

◆ ◆ ◆

THE NEXT MORNING, Alex waited to receive his payment before heading off to the corner of Bayard and Bowery. He enjoyed the walk, not just because he was bringing his first contribution to Waxey since coming back from the war, though that helped.

He stopped at one of the many stalls on Bayard and bought bread and a chunk of cheese nearby. The pleasure of making the purchase and consuming the simple fare made his cheeks glow red.

Inside Waxey's headquarters, Alex recognized Anthony on the door. His olive complexion and pointy nose hinted at his Italian ancestry. Charlie Lucky sure was tight with Waxey and Ira. He might only have been absent a year, but the landscape of the Lower East Side had completely changed. None of the old Irish and German gangs had survived the onslaught of the Italian arrival and where they worked with the Jews, money appeared to fly out of the storm drains.

Onto the first floor and a rat-a-tat until a voice signaled for him to enter. Alex nodded at both Waxey and Ira sat in their usual seats with a coffee each in front of them. A boy stood in the corner, hands behind his back, just like Alex had done when he'd first arrived in Waxey's orbit.

As Alex sat down he stretched out a hand and placed a roll of green into Ira's palm. He counted the notes, smiled and whispered the amount to Waxey.

"Welcome back, Alex. Feel good to be earning again?"

"Yep. Back in the land of the living. Or rather, I'm getting there. I still get flashbacks and that darkness hangs over me until I eventually shake it off…"

"Don't be so melodramatic. You survived the war and you'll survive the peace. All you have to do is recall one simple truth…"

"…We live together, we fight together, but we die alone. Waxey, you don't need to remind me and I am grateful for all you've done for me."

"Have a rest. I understand you are not fit yet. That is not a criticism, merely recognition that you deserve some recuperation time. By the new year, we will enter a different world. The Protestants convinced the president to ban the sale and consumption of alcohol. Charlie has some great ideas and so do I. Together we will take over the world—and you can help us if you're well enough."

Alex wished to find out more but knew better than to ask. When the time was right, he'd be fully briefed. The only problem was Alex's place wasn't to be on the receiving end of Waxey's plans. He wanted a seat at the table where the planning happened. Perhaps Waxey's new world might offer Alex opportunities to step up inside the gang.

9

ALEX DID EXACTLY what he was told and popped back to the Mercury, remaining at his table until the evening customers began to pile in. Then he winked at Uriel and slunk home still tired from the previous day's exertion. Threatening an unarmed woman had been more energy-sapping than he might have imagined.

Just as he entered the Oregon bar, he stopped and balanced himself with a nearby table. White light across his vision. A deafening zing split his head open and then his sight returned to reveal a stranger's face melted into his skull beneath an army helmet.

He closed his eyes, swallowed and raised his eyelids to see a roomful of drinkers and two nafkas leaning at the counter in search of a fresh john. A zigzag to the bar and Alex downed a shot of vodka in a single glug. He left a quarter on the counter and wended his way to the stairs and off to his room.

Sarah sat at her dressing table with a hairbrush in her hand. He walked over, kissed her on the forehead and then fell back onto the bed. She turned her head at the sound of his body hitting the covers.

"You all right?"

"Good enough. The war's still haunting me."

She put the brush down and sat next to him, a palm on his chest as a sign of comfort, but Alex felt no better. The images were one thing, but what really drove him to the edge were the relived emotions. The fear and panic in the pit of his stomach. No matter how long the fighting lasted—a minute or a day—that dread took root for the duration.

◆ ◆ ◆

SARAH LEFT ALEX inside himself and then returned to brushing her hair. Thirty minutes later, he woke up and stared at his woman silhouetted by a streetlight. The dark cloud in his mind had evaporated and instead he soaked in the beauty before him.

"You left me."

"I'm back now."

"For how long, though?"

"I don't know what you mean. There's nowhere I'd rather be than with you."

"But you walked out on me before, so how can I know you're not off again whenever you fancy?"

"I'm not the man I used to be. The war put paid to that."

"You're different, I'll grant you that, but you've been in the neighborhood a few months and now you're back under Waxey's influence, doing his bidding. At some point, you'll need to escape again. That's fine for you but I don't want to invest my time creating a life with you if you could vanish at any moment. I tried being patient with you while you got Rebecca out of your head and all that gave me was an empty bed and countless nights crying into my pillow."

Alex thought for a minute. She was right; he'd treated her so poorly. When push came to shove, he'd kept her at a distance. Her last memory of him must have been a kiss on the lips that morning and the sight of him bumping into Rebecca.

"I'm sorry. I was a selfish man, but I promise you I will stay true. You are my rock—the only person in the world who has offered me any genuine affection. You've been loyal when I haven't deserved it and tended to my physical needs when I was almost dead. I can never repay the debt of gratitude I owe you."

"Alex, I want to believe you but what have you offered me in the past? Empty words, ten dollars left on a bedside table and dust at your heels when you walked away."

"Whatever I said to you, I meant at the time and I never lied. If you remember, I said I couldn't commit to you because my head was filled with Rebecca and you told me you would wait and spend the rest of your life with me if I tired of yearning after that woman."

"Shall I strip off and get into bed because you make me sound like a whore? Lying around until her john gives her some attention and cash."

"Don't say that. I never treated you like some nafka. Respect— that's what you have always got from me. I am not those other men. You are my companion, my friend, my lover. You are my everything and I do not want us to be apart."

"Cheap words, Alex, because you left me to fight in a foreign land. And for what? *Gornisht*. Nothing."

Alex had not been expecting this onslaught and couldn't figure out what had caused it. He had come home for a rest, not an argument, and he was doing his best not to let his temper get the better of him.

"I thought I was saving the Jews who hadn't made it to America."

Sarah snorted and stared out the window.

"You put your life at risk for the goyim. Strangers."

"Monk Eastman…"

"…is a decrepit man, punch drunk, who'd hit the skids before you met him. Why did you listen to that *fercockte meshuggener*?"

He shrugged, sat up and swiveled his legs off the bed. She was right. Eastman had made sense at the time but only because Alex had wanted an excuse to flee his problems with Sammy in the Bowery.

"Well? Is this your idea of how to treat your companion? Silence."

"I'm not saying anything because you are right. I made a terrible mistake and have paid the price by nearly dying several times, and I almost lost you. I am sorry, Sarah. All I can offer you are my words and the hope that some day you will forgive me."

"Come here, you lummox."

She opened her arms and Alex stood in front of her and they hugged. Not the casual hug of occasional friends, but the deep comforting caress of two people who care deeply for each other even if they don't have the words to express it.

◆ ◆ ◆

ALEX AND SARAH ate at the bar having given themselves some time to calm down.

"We should do something special instead of just spending another night here, Sarah. Where would you like to go?"

She smiled and giggled. One finger twirled her hair around itself while she considered her options. She untangled her digit and stroked it along Alex's arm.

"Can we see a show?"

"Anything in particular, hon'?"

"No, something with a few songs and laughs."

Alex's knowledge of the theatrical world was extremely limited. He'd only been inside a playhouse once, when he first came to New York and had been couriering opium packages around town for Waxey, and he had delivered a brown parcel to Ida Grynberg at The Grand on Second and Tenth Street.

A quick check of his watch, and they grabbed a taxi to the theater. At the box office, they had ten minutes before the show started—a vaudeville revue featuring the world-famous diva that Ida had become. They settled into their seats in the stalls and a minute later the curtain rose. The opening act was a big musical number to wake up the crowd, followed by a comedy double. And so on.

Alex and Sarah sat one hand in the other's lap for the entire first half, only separating to clap the performers.

"We should do this more often, Alex."

"I didn't know such things existed. We never had this in the old country."

"You can take the boy out of the Ukraine…"

THE AUDIENCE ROSE and applauded when their beloved Ida opened the second half. She stood alone on stage at the start of her song and as the emotion and drama built up, she was joined by the chorus. Perhaps because his memory of Ida was of her shooting up in the dressing room, Alex was less impressed than anyone else in the auditorium and his eyes wandered around the stage.

For one instant, he thought he recognized a face and then it vanished into the back of the stage to emerge again two minutes later. Slightly older with longer hair, Alex reckoned he was staring at Rebecca Grunberg, the love of his teenage life.

His stomach tightened and a bead of sweat appeared on his upper lip. He wiped it away with his spare hand and hoped Sarah did not notice the change in his demeanor. All the good words he'd spoken that afternoon expressing his feelings for the woman by his side and one glance at someone who might be Rebecca had consigned it all to the trash. Or so it felt at that moment.

Alex blinked and tried to see his Rebecca for a third time but the song wound down and everyone exited the stage. He did his best to concentrate on the remaining acts but his mind returned to the memories of Rebecca practicing her ballet moves in her parents' apartment and of him at the door watching and marveling at her purity and beauty.

MARCH 1920

10

ON JANUARY 17, 1920 the world turned upside down with the arrival of the Eighteenth Amendment to the US constitution, usually known as the Volstead Act or Prohibition. Those who owned bars were the first to be impacted as there was not much money to be made selling coffee, although the brothels continued to make a roaring trade.

Illegal gambling was also unaffected by Prohibition because most people still believed they could beat the odds. Many johns had bought a couple of cases of beer or whiskey before the ban on the sale of alcohol had come into force but by the end of February many ordinary Joes were thirsty and, like everyone else on the wrong side of the law, Waxey saw an opportunity.

"Alex, this is the scoop. As you know, we've been shipping in rum from the Bahamas and while it sells, margins are tight and we see little long-term future in it. North is where the money lies."

"Upstate New York?"

"Canada, dear boy. We will drive whiskey over the Detroit river and bring it straight to our warehouses in the Lower East Side. The water is at its narrowest between Windsor, Ontario and Detroit, so that is where we shall cross the border. And because there's a river border, it's difficult for Uncle Sam to patrol."

Alex sipped his coffee and wondered why Waxey and Ira were giving him a lesson in economics. The three said nothing and Alex shuffled in his seat. A lifetime later, he decided he should break the silence before it overpowered them.

"Sorry, but why are you telling me about this?"

"Because you are fit and well now and we have a job for you and your crew."

Waxey smiled at Alex and glanced at Ira.

"We need someone tough we can trust to bring the shipment home, Alex. That's you."

His jaw dropped. Ever since Prohibition had been announced, talk across town had focused on how to make money out of this *goyishe* nonsense. Here was the answer.

"Get your men and head off to Windsor. You do this right and we'll look after you well. The days of running a street gang will be far behind you."

"Brilliant. Thank you... what's the catch?"

Waxey was the first to laugh, quickly followed by Ira, his old business partner.

"I like your attitude, dear boy. Straight answer to your straight question—you can end up dead. The Canadian and US customs will shoot you on sight if they find you smuggling liquor across the border. Then there are other interests—inside and beyond the Lower East Side who want control of this supply line and who'll do their damndest to stop you."

"Anybody else looking to see me dead?"

"Not that we've noticed."

"Better get started then."

VANNI BORGNINO SAT behind his desk and busied himself with some papers as Alex approached him. The guy looked up, smiled and reached out a hand to greet him.

"Any problems coming up here?"

"None. The border was quiet, and we pretended to be tourists. Is everything set this end?"

Borgnino was a stocky man but Alex wasn't about to underestimate him. If Waxey trusted him with an entire shipment of whiskey, the fella must be on the up and up.

"Pretty much ready. We are waiting on another six guns and then we can go."

"When are they due?"

"Tonight. Unless your men need a longer rest, I'd prefer to leave as soon as possible."

"Why the rush?"

"Not so much a rush as I'd like to get some kind of edge. Everyone knows everybody else's business, so we assume that word has got out about our travel plans. I have loudly told anybody within earshot that we are leaving tomorrow."

"I have heard there could be trouble along the way."

"And then some. The cops have informers and know we are going to take a shipment over the border but they don't know where we will cross…"

"…because you haven't told anyone."

"But even a bunch of cloth-eared Mounties will be able to follow the trail of a dozen trucks traveling at high speed across their country."

"They'll want our heads on a plate."

"You betcha. And assuming we get to the river safe enough, the fun's only just begun. We do not control anywhere in Detroit."

"And we have little influence between there and downtown New York."

"So I hope you guys are ready because this will be one hell of a ride."

"We can take care of ourselves."

"Sure you can, but how many times have you protected twelve vehicles, their drivers and a cargo that's worth more than gold?"

"We come bearing sawn-off shotguns and a reputation in the Bowery. Some of us have experience of fighting on foreign shores and lived to tell our loved ones about it."

Vanni smiled and whipped out a bottle of whiskey and poured two shots. They clinked glasses and swigged their drinks down.

Another slug for the road and everyone was ready to blaze a trail through hell.

ALEX SPREAD OUT his men along the convoy, with Paulie leading the trucks and the rest of the gang two or three vehicles apart with Alex himself in the rear. He considered putting himself in the first pickup but decided it was better to see everything that happened.

The only thing in their favor that night was the new moon. The pitch black which enveloped the convoy made seeing the road difficult although they banked on the Mounties having an equally tricky job of spotting them.

Vanni stayed with the trucks until they set off from the far end of Dougall Avenue, two miles away from the river and the American border. Under cover of the inky darkness, Alex and the crew kept their eyes sharp and trained on the road ahead and on the tree lines to the left and right.

Five minutes later, a motorbike zoomed out of nowhere and Alex nearly blew a hole in the rider's chest, but fortunately held back half a second because it was Paulie. With the trucks still forging ahead Paulie warned there was trouble ten blocks in front. Despite Vanni's best intentions, word had got out and a local gang was waiting to intercept them.

Alex hopped onto his truck's tailboard and jumped behind Paulie on the bike.

"Hit the gas, Paulie. We need to show these hobos not to mess with the Bowery boys."

The wind buffeted Alex's face as Paulie drove them ahead of the convoy and toward the locals. If Alex strained his ears, he could hear the engines of the convoy less than a minute away to their rear. While time was against them—there was no opportunity for a complex plan—the stupidity of their opposition fell in their favor. For no obvious reason, the gang had positioned itself under streetlights with two men behind each car and maybe three stationed on the corner of each building at the junction. There was no time to even count heads accurately.

"Let's do this."

Paulie and Alex jumped off the bike and split up, one on each sidewalk, then scurried along to get close enough to be sure their shots would cause maximum damage. When he got so near that he thought he could see the whites of their eyes, Alex squeezed the trigger on his shotgun and caused a large and bloody hole to rip through the chest of the nearest guy to him, but still two hundred feet away.

The gang responded with a hail of bullets but they had no real idea where the attack had originated—just somewhere up ahead. Paulie took out a pair on the corner and Alex knocked out three behind one car. The sound of the convoy had become a roar.

MORE SLUGS WHIZZED past and a pane of glass shattered behind Alex's right ear. He responded by ducking down for a second and pumping three slugs into his assailant's body. It crumpled to the floor and Alex tried to figure out how many were left.

Paulie took out a handful more as Alex totted up the living among the carnage. As the lead truck came to a stop next to him, Alex saw a solitary gunman with his hands above his head.

"Paulie, take a look-see and let me know when the area's clear. Everyone else, stay inside."

The barrel of his shotgun aimed squarely at the guy's heart, Alex strode toward the dude until he was only ten feet away.

"Where are the others?"

"Please, don't kill me."

"Answer my questions and you will walk away from this and have a tale to tell your grandchildren."

"There are no others. You've slaughtered all of us."

A shot rang out, echoing between the sides of the nearby buildings. Alex clasped his piece tighter.

"You lied. Are there any more?"

The guy's eyes were wide and fear oozed out of every pore. He'd been banking on that other fella to get reinforcements. Alex walked forward until the barrel pressed against the fella's chest.

"Talk to me, little man."

"There are none left here. Frankie was the last one."

"Where was he heading?"

"Back to our headquarters on the other side of town… I got a wife and kids…"

"How long before they get off their tucheses and pay us a visit?"

"Ten, fifteen minutes. You weren't expected until tomorrow so we didn't have much time to get ready. But the others will be over soon."

Alex smiled, pulled the trigger, and the guy's body flew backward with the force of the bullet scorching through his flesh. Ezra and Massimo arrived to clear the cars from the street and the convoy trundled through Windsor and headed for the river.

As Ambassador Bridge came into view with its twinkling lights, they turned left to avoid the customs post on the Canadian side. Half a mile later, they took a right onto Morton Drive and reached a large sandy area in the middle of nowhere.

Moored at the water's edge was a wide flat-bottomed boat, big enough for all the trucks. Alex's guys jumped out of their vehicles and maintained a line surrounding all this activity, facing outward, shotguns in hands. A silence fell all around as everybody's ears were keenly stretched for impending trouble. The rest of the Windsor gang could appear at any moment.

The locals knew what they were doing and after ten minutes, the boat was loaded and Alex's crew boarded. A vessel that size was never going to be speedy, but it felt as though every inch took an hour. Eventually, the Canadian shoreline faded and Motor City beckoned on the other side of the river.

11

GUNS IN HAND, Alex and his crew were the first to get off the barge to protect the trucks as they disembarked and the drivers got themselves prepared for the long haul to New York. Twenty minutes after the boat sailed back to Canada, everyone was ready to hit the road.

Just before Alex called for the first truck to begin, he saw a light in the distance. The speck of white got bigger until it became two dots and fifteen seconds later, the two dots became four and four became eight until Alex heard engines approaching.

"Get ready!" he warned, but they all knew this was make or break; the Windsor gang was only the start. The vehicles neared and Alex saw a guy on the tailboard of each car. Then two hundred feet away, they stopped. One man opened a door of the lead saloon and walked toward Alex until he was fifty feet away. All the while, his hands pointed to the floor, palms open. His coat flapped in the breeze as he slowed to a halt.

"My name's Abe Bernstein. Is Alex Cohen with you?"

Alex stepped forward and raised a hand.

"What brings you to this piece of dirt?"

"Waxey Gordon. Does his name ring a bell?"

"I reckon. You with the Sugar House gang?"

"Yep. Waxey mentioned you might be popping by."

The men walked toward each other so they didn't have to shout and could have a more private conversation.

"You're traveling through our territory so the least we can do is to see you have safe passage."

"Much obliged."

"We have received a consideration from Waxey so don't be so grateful."

"It's still good to see a friendly face, especially if this is the first of many runs."

"Let's not get ahead of ourselves."

"No, sure thing…"

Abe took Alex and the entire convoy to a secluded warehouse a few minutes away from their crossing place. This gave them an opportunity to freshen up and grab a bite to eat. With only two hours driving done, the worst of the journey was before them.

There were locked iron gates at the entrance and a pair of fellas carrying machine guns. That was security enough. Once within the confines of the building, everyone was given free rein although Alex stayed with Abe rather than gorging himself on food and women like most of the men.

"Waxey speaks highly of you, young man."

"Kind of him. Your reputation speaks for itself."

Alex was being polite. The Sugar House gang had made a name for themselves in Detroit as a hard-nosed bunch of fellas who ruled their territory with a ruthless determination and a large dose of chutzpah.

What none said but everyone knew was that they were lucky to be living in Detroit. Its location so close to the Canadian border made it the ideal spot to haul liquor into the US. And whoever controlled that town would dip their beaks into every bootlegging run. Abe understood it, New York knew it and Chicago wanted a piece of the action too. Everybody wanted to be friends with Abe and his brothers. Waxey had briefed Alex well. The two men jawed over a coffee and a bowl of chicken soup. Then he checked the time and decided they should get going.

"The new moon'll help us stay invisible tonight before we have to peel off the main road at dawn. The longer we last without attracting the attention of cops or local hoods, the better."

"My men will accompany you out of the city and then you're on your own."

"I appreciate all your support. We've got twenty hours driving ahead of us and we'll barely have time to stop for a piss along the route."

"Good luck—until we meet again."

ON THE ROAD, they stopped for a five-minute break every two hours which gave the drivers a chance to rest their eyes and his men seized the opportunity to stretch their legs. No one wanted to be cooped up inside those vehicles for that long.

Physical discomfort was the least of their worries. Even though Alex had planned a route away from anything like a main highway, word was out that a convoy was heading east and there was a greeting party in every town they tried to skirt past.

Waxey had given Alex simple instructions: pay off as many guys as he could but those who were not motivated by money or who didn't see reason should be shot on sight. Alex did his best to keep his bankroll in his pocket, preferring to fight than hand over any green.

As they avoided the cities, the only trouble that came their way was from smaller gangs and an occasional family that ran a town. Alex figured that if he was going to make this trip on a regular basis, then he didn't want to pay off some goyishe hoods every time their trucks rolled by.

Besides, Waxey had been vague about Alex's cut so keeping some of his boss's spending money was an easy way to make some gelt out of the jaunt. He'd deal with the consequences of disobeying Waxey if they got back in one piece. Handling the yokels was one thing. They had to force their way through New Jersey and then across downtown Manhattan before they could raise the flag of victory.

ONCE THEY SAW the first road sign for Jersey City, everybody relaxed. Everyone apart from Alex who knew the worst was yet to come. The Elizabeth family controlled a huge swathe of New Jersey, headed by Stefano Badami, a mean fella who was as tough as the reputation that preceded him. To top it all, there was bad blood between Waxey and Badami as they'd been vying for supremacy ever since Waxey had fallen in with Charlie Lucky.

The outskirts of Jersey City beckoned in the mid-afternoon sun and Alex wondered if they should take a detour further north but realized this would only burn more gas and not solve the fundamental problem that they were thundering through Elizabeth territory without permission.

So he kept to his original plan and aimed for Weehawken which had a ferry terminal, although Alex wasn't intending to take the liquor on to Manhattan using official means of transportation. Paulie's bike pulled up next to Alex, and he warned there was trouble ahead.

"There's a welcoming committee of around thirty guns. Time to find an alternate route."

"Any suggestions?"

"Make a run for it north. You'll find a bunch of derelict buildings a quarter of a mile in that direction. We could barricade ourselves in and defend ourselves from there."

"And then they can pick us off one-by-one. No deal. I've got a better idea but I'll need one brave soul to pull this off."

"You looking straight at me?"

"You volunteering?"

"Apparently so."

Alex outlined his plan and Paulie hopped into the lead truck. Its engine roared as the driver over-revved and it sped off aiming directly at the Elizabeth gang. As soon as the vehicle's smoke had cleared, the rest of the convoy zoomed south.

Two minutes later, they heard a volley of gunfire and then silence. Alex spat three times for luck and made a mental note to look after

Paulie's family when they arrived home—assuming they made it back in one piece.

The trucks trundled along the residential roads on the edge of the city. They were only a handful of minutes away from a confrontation with the gang. Each revolution of the truck's wheels took them closer to a bloody end.

More gunfire in the distance. Alex couldn't tell quite from which direction it came or how far away either. But if the gang was still shooting, then Paulie was alive and drawing the Elizabeth crew away from the convoy. They turned a corner and screeched to a halt. The road was blocked by three large trucks and at least ten fellas waving machine guns. There was nowhere to go except to meet your maker.

◆ ◆ ◆

ALEX HALTED THE convoy and swallowed hard. The Elizabeth gang were eight hundred feet away but there was no way the trucks could turn around and flee before being caught by the faster Elizabeth cars. Stand and fight was the only option.

He heard Abraham and Ezra's footsteps with Massimo trailing behind them. By the time all three reached him, Alex had hatched a plot. With a pair of binoculars, he counted the enemy numbers, twice.

"Listen real carefully. They know we are here and they can afford to wait. Remember, they want the liquor, not us so they will keep their eyes fixed on the trucks. We'll send one truck slowly down the street and they will assume it has come to negotiate. They won't shoot up the booze else they'd have ripped us to hell by now.

"Meantime, you three make your way along the street. Take your time. It's more important you get close enough to do some damage with your shotguns than blast at them ineffectively. Our truck will stop four hundred feet from the Elizabeth gang and you will not fire until I give the signal."

"What is it?"

"Ezra, when one of theirs collapses on the ground with a bullet between his eyes then keep firing at them all. Chances are the only thing you guys do will be to cause confusion, but that's precisely what we need to improve our odds. I'll do the rest."

His men spread out and scattered along the sidewalks, ducking and diving behind streetlights, parked cars and anything else that gave them protection from being seen by the machine gun toting Italian crew.

Alex grabbed a rifle from his truck, ran behind the nearest building and scaled the fire escape to reach the roof. His pockets were stuffed with shells, and he made his way from rooftop to rooftop until he was close enough to pick a vantage point where he could aim his scope at the heads and hearts ahead.

Thirty seconds later, their truck stopped on its cue and Alex watched the Elizabeth gang turn to each other as they wondered what was going on. He inhaled deeply and gave them his answer when he squeezed the trigger and a fella in a fedora fell down, crumpling onto his knees.

A burst of gunfire scorched across the nine remaining men, slugs ricocheting off their cars, windows shattering and mayhem all around. They responded by strafing anywhere in front with bullets, but Alex could tell the guys had no idea where to aim.

Another shell flew from the barrel of his rifle and a second fella discovered a new red hole in his body. And so this continued with Alex-the-marksman taking the kill shots while his Bowery men gave him the perfect cover. With only one fatality on their part, the East Side crew had done well, but that still meant Abraham's lay face down in a gutter. Two minutes after their truck had rolled into position, the Elizabeth crew lay in a bloody pool of their own liquid.

"Ceasefire!"

The four-second silence was punctured by whoops from the drivers. A quick check on the bodies to make sure no one was left alive, and they continued on their way to the Weehawken waterfront where two boats were waiting to transport the whiskey across the Hudson.

On the other side, the trucks sped across town until Alex recognized the streets. They were back in the haven of the Lower East Side.

12

WHEN HE GOT back to the Oregon, he took a shower to wash the grime of the interstate roads off his skin. Then he sat with Sarah at the bar and enjoyed a coffee. This was no ordinary hot drink as it was laced with a double shot of whiskey. It was known as an Oregon Coffee to those who frequented the joint regularly.

"You look tired, Alex."

"Like you have no idea, my *shayner maidel.*"

"Was it bad out there?"

"Had its moments, but we all got back in one piece, unlike some of the fellas we met on our travels."

Sarah shrank slightly away. She tried not to think about Alex's business too hard. She was occasionally on the receiving end of violence in her line of work and she avoided it at all costs for obvious reasons. On the other hand, bloodshed was drawn to Alex like flies to a midden and he usually shrugged it off casually. His manner showed her how tough this trip had been.

Alex was touched by Sarah's recoil. She might act as though she had a heart of stone but she was far more fragile than she would ever reveal in public. He reminded himself that his efforts to become somebody in this town were so he could take Sarah with him. She was his rock and his crutch. He needed her to get through the day, especially during difficult times like the ones they were living in.

"I'm glad you're back, safe and sound."

"It's great to see you; I'll be secure in your arms again tonight, hon'."

"So pleased to hear it, but I've got to warn you that you won't be happy in a minute or two."

Now it was Alex's turn to sit back as he girded himself for whatever bad news was going to descend from Sarah's mouth.

"I saw your mother this morning."

He couldn't decide if the world started spinning round or if he misheard.

"Mama?"

Sarah bit her lip, eyes gazing downward, and she nodded.

"Mama came here? To this place?"

"Oh no. We bumped into each other a block from here when I was out buying some food."

Alex understood this was no accident despite what Sarah thought. Ruth Cohen would not have wandered into this part of town just to purchase a slab of cheese. They might only be a handful of blocks away from the Cohen apartment but they were worlds apart and his mama understood that.

Besides, Alex hadn't spoken to her since the night before he left for France. In fact, he hadn't seen his father, Moishe or his brothers and sister either—apart from that moment when he'd watched them from afar in a near-dead funk. Esther would have grown up to be a woman by now and the little ones' ages probably cracked double digits.

"How are they all?"

"Fine, so she said... but she worries over you. Have you thought about visiting her?"

"Yes and discounted the idea. I can't imagine they'd want to meet this lump of disappointment again."

"She's your mother and she still cares about you."

"Or is it how much my business drags down her reputation in the community?"

"You're lucky you have a mother to worry over you and who's brave enough to walk down these streets of shame until she found me."

"Why now, do you think?"

"You are asking the wrong person. Pop over to Ruth and you'll find out."

"I'm not sure…"

"Listen, Alex. You have two options. Buy a challah tomorrow and visit them for a *Shabbas* meal or I'll drag you over there myself right now and you can deal with your mama's embarrassment at having a nafka grace her home."

"You don't leave me any option."

"Better believe it, pal. Watching you be apart from your family hurts me inside because I don't even know if my parents are alive or dead. You are a lucky man and are totally unaware of it."

Alex's cheeks warmed, and he agreed to buy some bread on the way over the following evening. He thought he might get some strudel too.

"Shall we go upstairs?"

"Does talk of your mother make you want to sleep with me?"

Sarah chuckled at Alex's expression, a mix of shock and confusion. They finished their drinks and returned to their room. Alex rolled over in bed as soon as he got under the sheets and was sound asleep, snoring loudly after a long, hard couple of days on the road.

ALEX STOOD ON the corner of Grande and Suffolk staring up at the tenements before him. They looked the same as every other bedraggled building on the street with its overcrowded apartments and the sounds of Jewish life zipping through the air on Friday night. But this tenement was special; on the fourth floor lived Moishe and Ruth Cohen, Alex's parents. He gripped the challah tightly and entered.

A slow walk up the stairs and memories of the smells and colors fogged his brain. Alex had forgotten quite how many steps there were and took a quick rest on the third floor right by the Grunberg apartment. He thought about the number of hours he'd stood in the open doorway admiring Rebecca's twists and turns. For a second, he glimpsed inside to spy on her parents, Max and Rosa, intoning blessings at the start of their meal.

Just before he thought he might make eye contact with them, he moved on to the fourth floor and the place he'd called home from the time his family arrived in the land of opportunity to the day when he left to join the army. Even as he said these words to himself, they were a lie. For months before he went off to fight, he'd been spending his nights with Sarah and only coming back to this place for a dutiful Friday night meal.

Alex knocked on the door and listened intently to the muffled voices and sound of shoes on wood as somebody approached. As the man opened the entrance, he spoke without looking up.

"Whatever you're selling, we are not buying."

As his eyes made contact with Alex, Moishe's jaw dropped and his arms slumped by his side.

"Who is it, then?"

His mother's voice floated to the entrance where the two men stood. Alex pushed the challah into Moishe's hand and rushed on through. With no idea what to say, he chose simple actions instead. His mother screamed at the sight of her prodigal son and Alex was home.

As he stepped into the front room, the younger kids stared at him while sister Esther stood up, sashayed over and gave him a hug.

"So good to see you again. We were told you were dead and paid for a grave and everything."

With those words ringing in his ears, Alex stepped toward his mother and planted a kiss on her cheek. This act of love extinguished her screams, and she began to sob at a much lower volume. He turned round to give Papa a handshake, but the man picked his jaw off the floor and followed Esther by giving him a lingering hug. A solitary tear rolled down the old man's cheek. Alex had never seen him cry before.

Then he felt hands pushing them apart and there was Mama wanting her turn to embrace him. The kids remained in their seats and chewed their bread, not knowing or caring about this stranger.

"Sit down—unless this is a flying visit."

"No, Mama. I'm hoping you'll let me stay for dinner."

"And why wouldn't I want my eldest child to break bread with the rest of his family?"

Alex shrugged and waited until Esther sorted out a chair for him as Mama shuffled the kids round to make enough space at the table. Only when he was sat down did he notice how quickly he slipped back into speaking Yiddish.

The family put their hands together, closed their eyes and Papa recited blessings over their food and drink. Alex recognized the sounds of the Hebrew words but understood virtually nothing that was said. His interest in religion had ended with the presents he received when he was Bar Mitzvah. And that was a lifetime ago in the Ukraine before they fled the pogroms.

A thousand questions descended on him and Alex had no idea who to answer first. So he opted for silence and eating instead. Then once everyone settled down, he spoke.

"Sarah told me you came looking for me, Mama."

"What's a mother to do when her own son goes off to fight, comes back and doesn't even bother to return home, check we are safe, enquire after our wellbeing."

Alex ground his molars and knew this was just her manner. Mama wasn't really angry with him. From what Sarah had told him, the woman was fraught with worry. This aggressive stance was her way of dealing with her mixed emotions—relieved to see him alive but annoyed he hadn't been round sooner.

"Things weren't easy for me when I first returned to America. Physically... and mentally..."

His mother dropped her silverware and covered her mouth with her hands.

"...but I'm fine now, more or less."

"Boys go to war but come back as men."

"Exactly, Papa. It took me a while to be at peace with what I'd lived through. And during that time I was too ashamed to let you see me, although I spied on you all one evening."

"We didn't see you."

"Even if you had, you wouldn't have recognized me. I was not in a good shape."

"Well, you look fit and well now, that's for sure. Pour Esther a small glass of wine, Ruth so she can join in the toast."

His wife did as Moishe bid and he raised the red wine in his hand, followed by the other adults.

"*Lekhayim.* To life."

A clink of glasses and everybody ate with Alex who was pleased to be accepted back in the family without further interrogation. Later when Esther and the other kids were clearing the table and washing the dishes in the kitchen, Alex and his parents had a more earnest conversation.

"Are you and that woman a serious item?"

"Yes, her name is Sarah and we care for each other. She nursed me through my darkest days and stayed beside me."

"You trusted that… woman more than your own mother?"

"She lives in a different world than you. I love you so very much and for that reason, there are some parts of my life I can't bring into this apartment."

"And you believe you can trust her?"

"I have trusted her with my life, Mama. Just because she was a prostitute doesn't mean she has no moral compass. Far from it."

"You spoke in the past tense. Has she vowed to stop being a whore?"

"Papa, she hasn't made a solemn promise to me, no. But she has been waiting for me for years and while we're together, I shall provide for her and she will have no need to obtain money from other sources."

His parents stewed on Alex's comments and he looked around the room. Every item of furniture—chairs, table, sideboard—were exactly the same as he remembered them. Nothing had changed one iota.

"What did you do with the money I gave you before I left?"

Ruth glanced to Moishe, who sighed.

"Your mother gave it all away."

Now it was Alex's turn to sigh. "That was to keep you safe."

"Didn't feel right, Alex. You know how we both feel about how you earned your living."

"I do—and that hasn't changed. Did any people pop over and check on you in my absence?"

"Yes and I sent them packing but every week they turned up with groceries, which was very kind."

"Did you accept the food?"

"I didn't want it to go to waste, but I never took the money."

Waxey had kept his word to Alex despite his mother's attempt to remain on high moral ground. This reminded him that somewhere in the city, probably on the Lower East Side, were bundles of cash hidden in a wall where he'd stuffed his hard-earned gains before he went off to war. He still couldn't remember where the hell he'd put it.

13

ALEX STAYED TALKING for another hour and then his mother began to yawn and Esther asked permission to retire for bed. He took that as his cue to go, but he promised to visit again as soon as he was able. He considered offering to host a meal at the Oregon but thought better of it. Back at the bordello, Alex joined Sarah at the bar and ordered an Oregon Coffee.

"How was your family?"

"Well, thanks. It was like nothing had changed all this time—apart from the fact that Esther, Aaron and Reuben were older. Especially Esther; she's become a woman since I've been gone."

"I'm glad you went. Family is important."

They clinked mugs and finished their drinks.

"You know something, Sarah?"

"What?"

"I learned a lot this evening, thanks to you."

"You're welcome."

She tilted her head to one side trying to figure out what he meant, but nothing appeared to come to mind.

"I know what's important in my life. Seeing my mother and father together content in their unhappiness. They help to keep the other on track. My mother with her perceived slights and prejudices. My father and his pompous belief in working hard and doing the right thing. One would be nothing without the other."

"Your mom seemed a bit lost when she was scurrying around the market yesterday—as though she was missing something."

"She was away from Papa and was not comfortable in these surroundings."

"Nicely put. She could barely bring herself to speak to me, a mere nafka."

"Let's not focus on that, please. Forget my mother for a minute, I've been trying to do that all my life."

They both laughed and Alex sandwiched Sarah's hand in his palms.

"I'm nothing without you and I don't want to lose you. In the dim and distant past, you told me you'd drop everything in your world to be with me. So tonight, I'm wondering if that's still true."

Sarah was silent. She smiled at him and soaked in the moment, but Alex realized he hadn't asked *her the* question and that was why she hadn't replied.

"Will you marry me, Sarah Fleischman?"

"Mister Cohen, I will."

JUNE 1921

14

FIFTEEN MONTHS LATER, Alex walked into the Richardson Hotel, holding its keys. Waxey had asked him to run the blind pig as a reward for shipping whiskey from Canada since the start of Prohibition. Now he'd passed on the day-to-day responsibility of the bootlegging to some Italian dude and was going to concentrate his efforts on this speakeasy.

There was more than one way to make money but Alex knew where the profit lay. And it was in those cups of laced coffee. Gambling and women were available for the unaccompanied man, but couples were welcome to just drink themselves under the table.

To keep customers entertained while they slurped, there was a stage with dancing girls singing their lungs out and a small house band to maintain the party atmosphere until the early hours. While Alex might not have been too familiar with many of the staff, one face shone through.

Alex recognized Nathan Milstein as the barman from his old haunt at the Forsyth, where Alex held court all the years he had used that cathouse bar for an office. Sammy and he had met there, and he'd cleaned himself in the backroom when there'd been too much blood to hide. He could trust Nathan with his life.

Alex wandered over to the counter and waited for Nathan to serve him.

"Waxey told me you'd be coming. What can I get you?"

"Straight coffee. I don't consume my own merchandise. Reckon that's bad business."

"You're right. Mighty glad to find you here. This dive needs a firm hand."

"Let's talk more after closing time. For now, I'll sit in a corner and watch how the place runs. Don't tell anyone about me."

Nathan nodded and took his drink to the back, away from the stage where Alex could monitor the bar and who went up and down the stairs for a spot of female companionship. He also checked out which customers were let into the adjoining room to play cards or take the roulette wheel for a spin.

AT THE END of the night, Alex had seen enough. He gathered everyone to sit at the customer tables and he stood on the stage so everyone could see him. First, he introduced himself and then he explained the new house rules.

"Just because the johns are tipsy, don't assume that I'm drunk too. When I work here, I am sober as a judge and there must be no skimming of any cash register. Please don't act aggrieved, I saw it happening throughout the evening and almost everywhere."

General murmuring as waiters, barmen, croupiers and nafkas all felt like they'd been personally accused. From what Alex had seen, Nathan was the only one of them who'd not dipped his beak in the trough.

"The next thing on my list is the games room. Many people are let in but appear to leave within a minute or two. We will not have timewasters in this joint. If we attract serious gamblers, then heavy drinkers will follow."

Alex kept his eyes trained on the doormen who he'd seen receive several tips just to be let in the room. He didn't mind people earning a living, but not at the expense of annoying hardened gambling men.

He surveyed the group of tired staff, who clearly would rather he had not walked into the Richardson at all.

"We will turn this into the most talked about speakeasy in the Lower East Side, if not Manhattan itself. Get with the program and you'll know riches beyond your wildest dreams."

"And if we don't?" asked a muffled voice somewhere near the back.

"Then you won't have to dream at all."

Once everyone else departed, Alex and Nathan walked round to check each room was ready for the next day's work. Just before they switched all the lights off, Alex offered Nathan a drink. They remained in a back room and Nathan took a bottle of whiskey out from a cupboard.

"What do you reckon, Nathan?"

"This place was being run into the ground. Chances are we'll lose people over the next week or two, but that's okay. You don't want thieves working for you."

"Do we get many highflyers visiting our gambling den?"

"I thought Waxey had told you all about this joint."

"Apparently not."

"About once a week, the Big Bankroll swings by and the house makes enough not to worry about who else plays cards for the rest of the time."

Alex's eyes opened wide. Waxey had neglected to mention that detail when he'd handed over the keys. He'd told him about the poor state of the whores and how he wanted Alex to sell more booze but he'd omitted to inform him that Arnold Rothstein gambled here.

THE RICHARDSON WAS located on Broadway and Twenty-sixth, just around the corner from Madison Square. Over the past year, with more than a little help from Charlie Lucky, Waxey had spread his wings north, out of the Bowery and toward midtown, leaving the Lower East Side behind him. He maintained control over every aspect of criminal activity south of Canal but there was a world of possibility away from the docks and piers.

While Charlie's reach was bigger than Waxey's, there were still areas which were not controlled by either of them and the

Richardson was two blocks away from the edge of Charlie's territory. Next door was Salvatore Maranzano's turf and ever since Charlie started working with Rothstein, Maranzano had been chiseling at the edges of his empire.

Two weeks after he pocketed the keys to the joint, Alex unlocked the main door as he always did in the morning. With his newfound responsibility had come a discovery of mornings, something he and Sarah had habitually avoided, preferring instead to enjoy the early part of the day in bed and asleep. They enjoyed their married life.

When Alex arrived at the entrance, he knew something was wrong before he'd even got to the door. To begin with, it was ajar, and he'd locked up tight the night before. As he stepped across the threshold, he drew his revolver expecting trouble.

There was devastation wherever he looked. Tables were upside down or smashed into pieces. The bar was a pile of firewood and the stage had deep axe gouges all over it. Gun still in hand, he headed to the games room—whoever had worked over the joint had spent time here. More tables strewn and destroyed and the four roulette wheels lay buckled on their sides on the floor.

A quick run up the stairs showed the bedrooms were in a similar state. Back downstairs, Alex went to his office. The door had been kicked in and was hanging on one hinge but nothing had been touched inside. Not a single piece of paper had been moved. That was a clear message.

This was no robbery by amateurs but a calculated attack by people who knew what they were doing and wanted to maximize impact— paperwork was not the target of this raid.

With the phones ripped out of their sockets, Alex went to find one that worked in a neighborhood store and told Waxey to send some men uptown. Then he waited until the fellas showed up and he organized them to keep watch at every entrance to the building.

Nathan arrived thirty minutes later and Alex told him the story of his morning.

"Get the word out on the street that we are closing for a refurbishment. We'll open again in a week come what may. In the meantime, I need to find Paulie and the rest of the crew. We've got an errand to run."

15

ALEX LAID OUT his plan to the boys in the Mercury and they asked questions until everything was clear. Then they downed their drinks and headed off to Maranzano's territory.

They walked north on First Avenue until the crew reached Twenty-sixth and on past the Richardson. Everyone put their hands in their pockets to keep a weapon on standby as they crossed Fifth then Sixth Avenue and reached Maranzano's turf.

The air tasted the same but the people on these blocks looked different. The massive reduction in Yiddish signs and language. More Italian spoken—and the clothes everybody wore. All these elements told the gang to stay tight and be ready for anything.

Pregnant with expectation for two more blocks, the crew straightened their backs at the sight of the Speckled Hen, a bar long-since vacated by Irish gangs at the turn of the century and now occupied by an altogether different clientele interested in a healthy mix of hooch and whores interspersed with an occasional bet on the turn of a card or the spin of a wheel. It was the Richardson with an Italian accent.

Thirty feet away from the entrance, Alex halted his gang, and they pretended to stop for a conversation. A fake laugh emphasized the ordinary state of this group of fellas if anybody had been bothering to notice them. They were just strangers in town, which meant they were potential johns but of no more interest than that to the casual observer.

The men entered the building and sat down at a table until a waiter swung by and offered them a drink. Paulie did all the talking as he had an authentic Italian accent, although the entire conversation was in English.

While the coffees were ordered, Alex scanned the joint. With a bar at the back end of the room and a stage on one side, there was an unmarked door which must lead to offices and an unknown number of guys with weapons. On the opposite side to the stage were drapes which Alex guessed led to the gaming area. One fella was all that separated them from the tables beyond the curtain.

"There's not much to see here. Paulie and I will pay a visit behind the scenes while you two play a few hands. Keep your eyes peeled but don't make any moves until we have announced our arrival. And remember, we are here to damage property and not to harm civilians. If anyone is going to serve up revenge, it's me, because the Richardson is mine."

Alex and Paulie waited near the staff entrance for fifteen seconds until they were certain no one had spotted them. Then they skipped into a corridor and closed the door behind them. There were muffled voices up ahead but they couldn't be sure quite where the noise came from. They pulled their revolvers out and slunk along the poorly lit space until they reached the far end and were faced with a choice between two doors.

Alex pressed his ear to both but the only sound came from the right-hand room. He signaled for Paulie to open the left-hand door and sure enough, there was nothing to see except filing cabinets and desks piled with papers. When they kicked open the other door, they were met by two surprised expressions belonging to a pair of fellas sat at a desk counting money.

Before they could respond by standing up or asking a single question, Alex had whipped the nearest guy around the chin with his pistol and Paulie had punched the other in the face. Paulie muttered something menacing in his native tongue and both fellas put their hands on their heads and kneeled on the floor.

A quick check of their pockets and the desk drawers revealed three pistols which Alex and Paulie stuffed into their pockets. Then Alex decided to clip the guys around the head because they had nothing to tie them up with and they would only be troublesome if they were allowed to wander the building. Paulie shrugged and he and Alex returned to the other end of the corridor and back into the auditorium.

EVERYTHING APPEARED CALM so Paulie and Alex wended their way to the gaming area. The fella in charge of the drapes eyeballed them but made no serious attempt to check them out. Poker was nearest and four roulette wheels were on the far side of the room. Cheap copies of Italian masters adorned the walls which had been painted a powder blue.

Alex saw Massimo and Ezra had separated and he caught their attention so they knew to be ready. Apart from the tellers who were unlikely to give them any trouble, there appeared to be just one fella running the room. Paulie sauntered over to be near him and Alex waltzed into the middle, halfway between the card tables and the spinning wheels.

He fired his gun into the air, causing a pile of fractured plaster to fall on nearby customers, who screamed in surprise at the sound of firearms and because it felt as though the ceiling was caving in. Alex fired again, and the gamblers stormed for the exit.

The nominal head of the room had been thumped at the base of his neck by Paulie as soon as the first shot left the barrel. Massimo and Ezra seized the opportunity to upturn tables, smash chairs and destroy green baize and roulette wheels as quickly as they could, transforming everything into firewood.

While the crowd continued to surge through the single door space, the four men joined the throng to hide among the johns. They reached the auditorium and scattered in separate directions. Two fellas stood in the middle of the room to calm down the mob spewing out of the building.

In less than a minute, the place was empty, apart from Alex's crew and a number of fellas who had appeared from a hidden door in one wall. Suddenly this was no longer a fight Alex thought they could win as they were clearly outnumbered.

Seven guys spread themselves out around the room with Paulie, Massimo and Ezra feeling the squeeze before anything had even happened. Alex eyed all the dudes as best he could, trying to figure out who needed to be taken out first and how to wend his way through the table chicane to reach them.

The stand-off lasted half a minute until Paulie spoke in Italian using the most commanding voice in the world. All heads turned to connect the sounds bellowing across the auditorium with a head containing moving lips. And this was the moment Alex attacked.

He lunged at the nearest fella who was only ten feet away. As he rushed forward, dodging past two tables, he raised his pistol arm and aimed squarely at the guy's chest. Then Alex reached him and saved a bullet by slamming the gun into the fella's face. Blood spurted out of his nose and eye, causing him to drop to the floor in agony. A kick to the groin ensured he wasn't getting up soon.

On cue, the other three zigzagged around the white linen-draped obstacles and punched, gouged and pummeled their way through as many of the guys as they could. In less than a minute, three of theirs were felled, and the match was even.

Everybody stopped for a second to take stock. Ezra glanced at Alex and smiled, pleased with their efforts. Then a crack splintered the air and Paulie flew over a table, spraying a red arc onto the tablecloth. He was dead by the time he landed on the floorboards.

ALL THE MEN hit the deck and Alex pushed the nearest table over as bullets started to fly across the room. Massimo popped up his head for a moment and seized the opportunity to aim a slug into one of the Maranzano gang.

Now there were three of them and three of Alex's crew so they had a chance, although Maranzano's fellas were in a better position. Alex's guys were nearer the center of the room and were facing off against men stood by walls so there was only one side from which they could be attacked. This wasn't going to be easy.

Another hail of bullets and Alex was pinned to the floor, face down. He heard the zing of a slug as it entered human flesh but had no idea who had been hit. A quick check to the side of his hiding place and he just about made out a body slumped to his left: one of the Maranzano goons.

"You guys good?"

Positive noises from Ezra and Massimo gave him cause to breathe easier for a few seconds. Italian spouted from Massimo and there was a moment's lull as whatever he'd said was given due consideration.

"What did you say to them?"

"I told them we made a terrible mistake and asked if they'd let us leave if we put down our arms."

"Seriously?"

"Why not? They're standing between us and the door, aren't they?"

Massimo was right. Alex had been so focused on attacking the men, he hadn't given a thought to how they were going to get out. He'd figured they'd walk out once the others were dead, but Massimo had calculated their odds differently. One fella shouted something back.

"The guy in charge—the one to the left—says we can walk free if we stop right now."

"That's mighty fine of him. Let him know we appreciate his kind and respectful consideration. Tell him we came here hot-headed from the Richardson and should have thought through our actions a little more clearly. We will pay for the damage to his premises too."

As Massimo translated Alex's good intentions, Ezra scurried along the floor and under a table to get a better vantage point. All that remained visible were his feet sticking out. Alex checked the chambers of his revolver and found he only had four bullets left.

"Do your new friends understand any English?"

"Not that I can tell."

"And how's your Yiddish after all these years?"

"Nicht so schlecht."

"Then listen carefully."

Alex told Massimo and Ezra exactly what they needed to do if they were to triumph that afternoon. Besides, Alex knew that they would never be allowed to leave this place alive no matter what some blind pig boss might promise. Heroes or in a coffin—those were the only ways they would exit this building today.

From nowhere that Alex could see, a stream of bullets came flying over his head—the goon had got himself an automatic machine gun. With his lips almost sucking the ground, Alex counted pairs of feet through the table legs and realized that one more man had appeared through the invisible door. The machine gun must be his.

All they could do was wait for the onslaught to finish because so many bullets were flying thick and fast only a fool would have raised his head out from hiding just to get off a single lucky shot. After a minute, there was a sudden silence as the guy had to reload and then they grabbed the chance they'd been waiting for.

Massimo fired a shot into the shins of one fella, who dropped to the ground enabling Massimo to fire off two more slugs, but this time one entered the guy's chest and the other coursed through his eye and out the other side of his head.

Ezra rolled out from his hiding place and threw a knife into the neck of the goon with the machine gun. He spat out blood, gurgled and flew backwards. Alex hadn't known Ezra had brought a blade to this gunfight.

This left the boss who stood and stared as both his comrades fell within seconds of each other and Alex rushed towards him while he was focused on the destruction surrounding him. Alex squeezed the trigger but nothing happened; the mechanism had jammed. Instead he kept on running, hoping that the guy wouldn't expect him to do anything as crazy as he was attempting.

He reached the fella and landed an enormous punch to his chin before he had registered Alex was stood in front of him. Luigi fell to the floor with Alex sat astride him, punching and slapping him around the face until there was nothing left but a bloody mess. He carried on raining blows upon the corpse and only stopped when both Ezra and Massimo physically dragged him away and waited for him to calm down.

Once Alex had caught his breath, he surveyed the devastation. Blood sprayed on himself, the walls, floor and tables, along with enough bullet holes to use the plasterboard for a sieve. Dead bodies and destroyed drinking and gambling equipment. Paulie lay still surrounded by a red pool of liquid.

"Let's get him home—after we burn this joint to the ground."

16

THE NEXT DAY, Alex paced up and down the hallway in Waxey's headquarters all too aware that Ira and Waxey were talking about him on the other side of the door to their second-floor office. After an eternity, the hinges creaked, and they invited him inside.

As usual, they both sat in exactly the same location with almost the identical posture too. It was as if the furniture was so used to their weight and the position of their bodies that the wood had warped to match their lumps and curves.

Today there was one significant difference—a new fella sat with them, Benjamin Siegel. Thick jaw and haunted bugged-out eyes but nothing else out of the ordinary about him. Alex had seen him with Waxey before but had never been this up-close to the guy who was making a name for himself as a gun for hire. As Alex sat down, Benjamin rose, tipped his hat and left.

"See you around, Alex."

"Bye, Benjamin."

"Gentlemen..."

And he was gone. This left Alex being stared at by Ira while Waxey stirred the spoon in his coffee. This was pure affectation because the man never added sugar or cream so there was no need to have the spoon in the drink in the first place.

"Yesterday, some misfortune happened at the Richardson, dear boy."

"Yes and I heard that a speakeasy burned down on the other side of the tracks."

"That news came my way too. I assume they were connected."

"Stranger things have happened, Waxey."

"Was anyone hurt?"

"Not in the Richardson. Maranzano hit us overnight."

"And then you responded in the cold light of day."

"More or less."

Alex felt uneasy because he could not be sure what Waxey thought of the previous day's exploits. Should he have done nothing? Sought permission before acting? Kept Maranzano's crew alive?

"I would have done the same, dear boy, and my boss would have reprimanded me for not seeking permission before I had gone over there and blasted a hole in the head of every single one of them. How did you know the perpetrators were in the Speckled Hen?"

"I had no idea. It was the first Maranzano place we found. An eye for an eye, so it didn't matter to me which joint got blinded."

Ira snorted to hide his mirth and Waxey grinned.

"For the record, you should have come to me first and agreed a hit on Maranzano's territory. I have spent much of the morning preventing an all-out war from erupting. The good news is that they struck us first and we were only retaliating, although turning the place to ashes was hardly a like-for-like response."

"Sorry about that. I saw a red mist by the end. All those bullets flying brought back memories from less happy times."

Alex stared into the middle distance and Waxey gave him a moment to return from France to the Lower East Side.

"The good news is that Charlie Lucky interceded on our behalf and took the heat. We've done good business together over the last year or two, especially with booze..."

"...and prostitution."

"Yes, Ira."

Silence for a second as Waxey lost and regained his train of thought.

"So, Charlie spoke up on our behalf and smoothed matters over. We are fortunate because Charlie and Maranzano are rivals, but Lucky has fingers in so many pies that he can't afford for us to fight among ourselves. And he is right; there is way too much money to be made these days with hooch, gaming and women. You'd almost believe the days of union infiltration and protection were a thing of the past."

All three men laughed at that joke, because they understood that Waxey was the man who controlled every pier and every dock on the Lower East Side. There wasn't a union in the area that didn't pay a weekly subscription to the man.

"Seriously, Alex. Send a token of appreciation to Charlie for stopping this from getting out of hand."

"I'll also need to look after Paulie's family."

"Leave that honor to me. A small lump sum to his favorite nafka is not something with which you need to concern yourself. Focus on what is important. Aren't you expecting your first child sometime soon?"

"Today, Waxey. Sarah went into labor a few hours ago."

"Get over to the hospital then so you can stand idly by while she does all the work."

Alex nodded and rushed to leave. As the door closed behind him, he heard Ira's voice offer some practical advice.

"Don't forget to buy a large box of cigars. You are going to want to celebrate once she's done all her pushing."

MOISHE ISIAH COHEN was named after his paternal grandfather and what Sarah remembered being told was the name of her father. The labor had taken six hours and the little man screamed a lungful as soon as he entered the world—so much so Alex heard his first cries from the waiting room where he immediately handed out cigars to anyone willing to receive one. Ira had been right.

Over the following year, Sarah, Alex and Moishe did their best to learn how to be a normal family. They were so very happy. Of course, there were many occasions when Alex had to be away from home but he did his best to make sure he always looked in on his *bubbala* before he went to bed.

His relationship with Sarah ran the gamut of high pleasure—Moishe's first crawl, first word, first anything—through to harsh crises. While Sarah wanted Alex to succeed, she loved him too much to want to see him get hurt and she knew his work would kill him eventually.

For Alex, if Sarah wanted to enjoy the trappings of his success then she would have to accept that this much money came at a price. She told him she only wanted to be happy but she wore the fur coats with a little too much relish.

SMOKE. MUD. BLOOD. Sweat poured into Alex's eyes as he hauled himself out of his foxhole and up the slope toward Bobby. No more than five feet on, he hit the dirt as shells landed all around. His friend continued to scream in pain and that damn sniper had him pinned down so he could hardly move. Fear in the pit of his stomach knotted until tears dripped out of his eyes.

INSTEAD OF LIVING in a room above a flophouse, the Cohens had moved into an apartment of their own on Avenue A and Second. While still a rented tenement, it was a place of their own and the landlord was Ira. While Alex created sufficient wealth for him then the rent was never going to be something they'd need to hand over.

Alex didn't notice it, but for the first time in his life he knew some contentment. It wasn't happiness, because he spent the summer of '21 living through the daily grind of bootlegging, union bashing, running numbers rackets and organizing cathouses. But the peace he experienced at home was new to him and he enjoyed it more than words could say, despite the hours spent awake in the middle of the night.

Sarah shouldered the greatest share of the burden of looking after Moishe—changing diapers, preparing and feeding the little man—and Alex did the things he was most comfortable with. Playing with

Moishe after dinner if he was back in time or taking a family trip to Coney Island on an occasional day off.

The Cohens settled into a routine of domesticity with Alex the breadwinner and Sarah ruling the household. If he'd put his head above the parapet for even a second, Alex would have realized that he had become his father, although Moishe senior was a tailor and not a member of an organized crime gang.

As summer turned to fall, Waxey continued to tighten his grip on the flow of alcohol into the Eastern Seaboard—with no small help from Charlie Lucky and his connection to financier and gambler, Arnold Rothstein.

No major criminal activity on the East Coast took place without Arnold's approval because he was the go-to guy if you needed seed capital for any illegitimate venture. He had funded the first whiskey run through Detroit and had assessed the risks when Waxey and Maranzano had nearly gone to war. The man might have operated from the back of Lindy's Restaurant in midtown but he owned the world.

FEBRUARY 1922

17

AS THE IMPACT of the Volstead Act deepened, Waxey secured his position as the lynchpin of East Coast booze. High class and rich customers demanded quality product and Waxey obliged by ensuring safe passage for Canadian whiskey, authentic scotch and English gin. His long-time associate, Charlie Lucky worked with him on these supply lines.

Behind the scenes stood Rothstein, who was rarely mentioned but the movers and shakers knew of his presence. If there was a deal to be done or a business venture to make money, then the Big Bankroll had his manicured hand in the action.

Meantime, Alex no longer operated out of the back of a brothel. Nowadays he rented an office on Avenue B and Fourth with the name of a fake company on its glass door. Along with a desk and a potted plant, a coffee table, a couch and three easy chairs. All black leather.

A filing cabinet stood in the corner but if you'd taken a moment to open any of the drawers, you would have found them completely empty. Alex kept no records because none of his business dealings were legal and he saw no reason to create a paper trail for any nosy cop to find.

One cold Tuesday morning, Alex sat at his desk, while Ezra and Massimo hung around waiting for their men to report on the day's collections. The guys laughed and talked about nothing, and occasionally Alex would dive back into his newspaper.

A knock on the door made him look up and eyeball the other two. They both shrugged and Alex indicated for Ezra to get off his tuches to welcome their unexpected guest. Once all three were poised with a hand on their piece, Ezra let the visitor in. As soon as his face was revealed, they gave a collective sigh of relief—it was Benny Siegel.

Alex recognized him as one of Waxey's heavy-hitting associates who would drift out of view when Alex appeared.

"Come in and sit yourself down, Mr. Siegel."

"Call me Benny like all my other friends."

Alex walked round his desk and the men shook hands. Alex scooted Massimo out of his seat so Benny could remain close to his desk.

"Would you care for a coffee?"

"No, thank you. I'm good."

"Ezra, Massimo, would you be so kind as to pop out and buy me a cup of java?"

"Both of us?"

"That's right."

Alex scowled until they both got the message to leave so he and Benny could have a private conversation. Once they were gone, Benny drew a deep breath and described his problem.

"Waxey recommended we speak as I have a delicate matter and I need your help."

"What would you like me to do?"

"I have a friend in Chicago who has asked me to do him a favor and usually I would be happy to oblige."

"But not this time."

"My face is too well known in the Windy City and this matter requires a stranger. Somebody we can trust to do a good job who won't make a fuss and will move in and out of the city without causing a ripple."

"I'm flattered my public profile is so poor in the Midwest that you'd want to approach me for the task."

Benny smiled because both men understood Alex's position as the go-to guy on the Lower East Side.

"If I were to agree to offer my support, what would you have me do?"

"A simple act of persuasion. My friend is having difficulties maintaining his whiskey supplies from Canada because a certain individual is expanding his activities on the north side of town."

"You want me to go to Chicago to ask a guy to not block a whiskey convoy?"

"Insist, not ask."

"How strongly would I need to insist?"

"Whatever it takes to ensure the flow of booze into the south side."

They agreed Alex's fee with no negotiation as Alex understood this could be the start of a significant relationship and he didn't want money to get in the way. Also, he knew that Benny Siegel was not the kind to appreciate some gonif trying to haggle with him.

"Does your friend have a name?"

"Just ask for Alfonse."

Benny supplied an address and walked out, just as Ezra and Massimo returned with Alex's drink.

"What was all that about?"

"I'm going on a little trip."

THE REASON CHICAGO is known as the Windy City is lost in the mists of time. Many thought it referred to the Hawk Wind that squalls off Lake Michigan while others believed it was a reference to blowhard politicians from the previous century. Alex didn't care much about such issues. He wrapped his coat tight around his body as he stepped off the train. It was damned cold, and the breeze cut through him like a knife.

He was greeted at the station by a tall thin guy wearing a similar black coat and a fedora. Alex had never met him before but knew exactly who he was and followed the fella out of the station and onto the sidewalk for a five-block walk which led to a speakeasy. At the back was the entrance to a much larger room with gaming tables and girls aplenty.

The guy headed straight to a particular white tablecloth at the edge of the action and sat down. As Alex approached, the guy's eyes stared at another door and so Alex entered alone. Down a corridor and into a busy anteroom where fellas talked, moved bits of paper around desks, and generally appeared to be fiercely occupied.

With everyone ignoring him, Alex stayed at the entrance and waited. He knew he was expected and someone would have to deal with him otherwise he'd hop onto a return train sooner than planned.

Twenty seconds later, a plump man left his adjoining office to look at his people scurrying around like bugs. He took one glance at Alex in the doorway and pounded over to offer him a handshake.

"Come in. I hope they haven't made you wait too long. Nobody has any manners in this town."

"I'm Alex."

"Of course you are and I'm Alfonse Capone."

"I don't mean to be rude but how do you know I am who I say I am?"

"If you weren't, you'd be dead, young man. In case you hadn't heard, this is my town—or soon will be once you help me clear out the riffraff."

"Is there somewhere we could go that's more private? We have a few details to iron out."

Alfonse explained how difficult Alex's prey would be to kill while they sat in his office. They had slumped onto a massive leather couch and Alex sipped on a scotch on the rocks he'd taken more out of politeness than any desire for liquor.

"Brady Madden is no fool. He keeps off the streets most of the time and when he ventures out, he surrounds himself with foot soldiers."

"From what I read in the New York papers, the Chicago way involves the shooter swinging by in a car and letting rip with an automatic weapon. I wouldn't be hanging around street corners if I were Madden either."

"So how are we going to nail the Irish sonofabitch?"

Alex had a long hard think and hatched a plan that would enable him to kill the guy in broad daylight. He told Capone what he needed and took a swig of his drink.

"I like your thinking. I can see why Benny wanted to send you. You've got a long day tomorrow. I have organized some discreet accommodation for you. Would you like a skirt to keep you company?"

"Thanks, but I'm a happily married man."

"I didn't ask about the state of your marriage, but whether you wanted some tail tonight."

"I'm more concerned to know the food's going to be to my liking."

"No bacon or ham. I understand."

"That's not what I meant. I've heard strange things about Chicago pizzas."

Alfonse laughed and shook his head.

"Don't go believing everything you read in them papers. You can have a steak, some pasta or a nice piece of fish. Whatever you fancy."

◆ ◆ ◆

CAPONE WAS AS good as his word; Alex ate well and slept soundly. The housekeeper woke him up, and he hustled out of the joint without paying, because Alfonse had made clear he would take care of the bill for his East Coast guest.

A brown paper package had been left for him at reception which he collected before making his way to offices one block away from Madden's favorite daytime haunt. Alex's plan relied on Madden following his usual daily routine. So Capone had called off all the fellas he'd hired to keep vigil over Dean O'Banion's underboss.

Alex took the stairs up to the fifth floor and idled along the corridor until he reached the location Alfonse had found for him at very short notice. As promised, the door was unlocked, so he walked inside and locked it in case of any unexpected visitors.

Three windows overlooked the street with a terrible view of more buildings opposite. There were many workplaces with a more enjoyable aspect, but this was perfect for Alex. By standing next to the right-hand window, he had a clear line of sight to the joint where Madden was holed up.

The gangs in Chicago were populated by young guys who had not learned their craft on the battlefields of Europe or the mean streets of the Bowery. Instead they relied on the scattergun effect of a hail of bullets to mask the fact that their aim wasn't very good. Hence the need to drive by so close and the notoriety achieved by the Chicago mobs with so many civilians slain without an apparent care in the world.

Alex unwrapped his parcel and summoned up all his army training to see him through the day. Among all the paper nestled a rifle and scope with a box of slugs. There had been no time to organize a tripod to steady the gun but Alex dragged a low cabinet over to the window to rest his elbow and maintain a clean line between the barrel and the building facia some four hundred feet away.

Just as he had learned to do every day as a sniper on the Western Front, Alex kept both eyes open as he stared through the telescopic lens. Meanwhile, his first finger stayed away from the trigger in case an accidental twitch ruined proceedings.

Two hours later, he licked his lips for the hundredth time and regretted not bringing a drink with him. His stomach rumbled too, but he knew he couldn't quit his position. The moment he did that, Madden would leave and not come back for another day.

Alex scrunched up his face to take his mind off his hunger and thirst. When he opened his eyes, he saw Madden standing by his office window. Although the view was far from perfect, he recognized the guy from the description Alfonse had provided, right down to the mole on his right cheek.

One inhalation and Alex placed his finger so that the tip was touching the trigger. The crosshairs on the scope were aimed straight at Madden's heart and Alex prepared to fire. Then a flurry of movement and Madden was through the door, out onto the sidewalk and ambling toward him, flanked by four guards, two front and back, one left, one right.

Alex's breathing increased as he did his best to keep the barrel of the rifle moving to match Madden's pace. Trouble was that the goon in front of him always stood between Alex and his target. This was getting desperate. At any minute Madden could cross the street or a car could pull up and he'd get in and be gone.

Then Madden stopped and looked down at his feet. Loose shoelace? No idea, but nobody told the goon up front who carried on walking for two paces until he noticed he no longer had company. And those two steps made all the difference. With no one there, Madden was unprotected—as naked as the day he was propelled into this world, despite the three guns surrounding him.

Alex inhaled and squeezed the trigger as the air began to leave his lungs. A bullet landed neatly in the upper right sector of his torso and the guy fell backwards, bumping into the gun behind. The two fellas either side twisted round and whipped out their weapons, but they hadn't figured out where the assailant was hiding. Alex sent a second slug into Madden's head, making a hole in his chin and a red mess as it left the other surface of his skull.

With both shell casings in his pocket so he didn't leave the joint in an untidy state, Alex used a cloth to wipe down the barrel and other surfaces of the rifle. Then he returned it inside its brown paper packaging, shifted the cabinet to its original position and left the office via the stairs.

A crowd was rushing to the slain body nearby but Alex strolled in the opposite direction and deposited the package in a dumpster at the back of a hotel. Then a long walk to the station and a relaxing train journey home.

18

WHEN ALEX'S TRAIN finally pulled into New York, he went straight home to freshen up and change his clothes—traveling light meant wearing the same suit for three days in succession. Once he'd sat down with Moishe for a few minutes, Alex found Sarah and gave her a peck on the cheek. He placed his palm on her round belly and smiled.

"What have you got to be so happy about?"

"You look so beautiful when you're pregnant, hon'."

"Fat and ugly, more likely. Men have it easy. You swan in here having been God knows where the last three days and act as though nothing has happened. Meanwhile, I'm stuck looking after our son and sweating like a pig with the second bundle of joy coming our way."

"My work takes me places…"

"Tell me about it."

"We got you a housekeeper to ease your burden."

"You hired a maid I don't trust not to steal our silver."

"She's a thief?"

Alex ground his molars and stiffened his back.

"Rosa is fine. She's reliable and Moishe loves her… I've missed you, I'm tired and I want you to be home more. Even with the hired help, I still crave adult conversation. When you're away, I'm left with baby talk and a servant stuck in this small apartment."

"It felt big when we first moved in."

"Anything seems large compared to a single room in a flophouse, but the family is expanding. If you were home more, then you'd know for yourself."

"I'll see if Ira has a bigger place for us."

"Instead of receiving handouts from your friends, maybe you should get a place by yourself. I don't know what you get up to anymore and I haven't asked, but I understand that in your business everyone has their day. They shine and then they fade—and Waxey's star has been shining for years."

As much as he was annoyed with Sarah for climbing on his back as soon as he'd entered the apartment, deep down what she said rang true. The only trouble was that now was not the time.

"WE'VE BEEN TALKING about you while you've been away."

"Nothing too rude, I hope."

Waxey and Ira looked at each other and smiled as Alex sat down at his usual perch in their meeting room.

"That accommodation you made to Benny has got you attention all the way back here on the East Coast."

"Amazing how the New York papers covered another guy dying on the Chicago streets."

"It wasn't in the press. Not here. Benny Siegel was extolling your virtues to Charlie Lucky, who had a conversation with me."

"I'm surprised anything got done when I was away with all this talking."

"Don't be fresh. The work you did was a test of your mettle. Madden was an O'Banion underboss, so it is only fit and proper that one underboss is killed by another."

Alex didn't quite understand what Waxey meant. It had just been another hit. Nothing special.

"We are giving you control of all the Lower East Side operations—still reporting to me."

"Sure, Waxey... I mean, thank you. This is more than I ever dreamed possible."

The lie dripped off Alex's tongue because he wanted much more than the Lower East Side but this was a very good start and he needed Waxey's continued support.

"Show your appreciation by making us more money and doing favors like in Chicago. It takes a steady hand to shoot someone from a block away."

While Alex walked the men through the mechanics of what he'd done, the rest of his mind raced through what he had just been given. He was now responsible for all the drinking, gaming and women fraternization south of Fourteenth Street and east of the Bowery. Not to mention all the union and protection rackets.

He controlled the juiciest docks in Manhattan but even in his moment of triumph, Alex wanted more. He already had his eye on the area north of his neighborhood and wondered how he could take a bite out of the other side of the Bowery. How to eat into Maranzano's territory would wait for another day.

One of his first acts as underboss was to pay a visit to a house on Forsyth and Stanton, a short hop from his old haunt as a teenager. After a brief discussion with its owner, Alex acquired the deeds to the place overlooking the parkland, and the Cohens moved in before Moishe's brother David was born.

THE SUCCESS OF the Italian and Jewish gangs in New York and America's other major cities created a response from the authorities. Ordinary citizens looked to the police to do something about the scourge of crime which blighted the urban sprawls from east to west.

The Big Apple was not immune from this increased interest in upholding the Volstead Act and word on the street was that times were about to become a whole load tougher.

"What we need is to get an inside track on the department of booze."

Ezra and Massimo nodded agreement as they sat around Alex's coffee table in his paperless office, but they had no suggestions or ideas of their own to offer.

"There's too much money to be made out of bootlegging to let the cops destroy all that we've built up. Any of you got an in with any of the beat flatfeet round here?"

Silence and shaking of heads. Ezra scrunched his face as though he was concentrating hard but left Alex with a faint impression that he needed to hit the head.

Alex restated the problem: "Tammany Hall is funding a group of out-of-town shoe leather to find the stills and put us out of business."

"And the distribution. With enough men, they could impound our trucks and destroy the booze in our warehouses."

"Exactly, Massimo. So we need to do something now before they get out of hand." Alex let out a heavy sigh.

"We can't bribe or kill gumshoes if we don't know who they are," stated Ezra.

"And how are we going to do that then?"

Alex was getting annoyed because he'd thought his top fellas would be more attuned to the problem at hand. Every day there was some story about how the so-called department of booze was readying itself for a big push. The Bureau of Prohibition was closing in and Alex could feel them breathing down his neck. His surprise was that the other two couldn't sense the black shoes and shaved sideburns too.

"I might know a guy…"

"Ezra, I'm sure you do. Why should I care?"

"This one works in the police department in the day and plays poker at night. He's good at catching thieves but terrible at judging a hand of five cards. Given how much he owes me, I reckon he might be prepared to spill his guts. One more bad day and I was planning on rearranging his kneecaps, anyway."

"Don't lean on him too hard as he'll be more of use to us if he's not laid up in hospital. I'd rather we suffer the loss of a few hundred dollars…"

"…four thousand, Alex. I've been mindful to be generous…"

"…a few grand lost now could be enough to save our entire bootlegging operation. That's a trade worth making. Let's pay a visit to this gentleman and see what we can agree.

◆ ◆ ◆

EZRA AND ALEX waited at the back room of the Stars and Stripes, one of the many speakeasies under Cohen control. It was way too early for a cop to come calling so they spent an hour reminiscing over old times and propping up their optimism for the future despite the dire circumstances the operation was facing.

Then Ezra nudged Alex and shifted his glance to stare at a guy in brown pants and a white shirt. And a haircut that screamed cop. They waited for him to settle into his seat and sip his Irish coffee before they sauntered over and Ezra made the introductions, Ezra flanked to his left and Alex to his right.

"How's Lady Luck, Frankie?"

"Some you win, some you lose. You know how it is."

"Lately it's not been much of a winning streak, has it?"

"Not so's you'd notice, but every hand is a fresh chance to win, right, Ezra?"

"Spoken like a true winner."

"I wonder if you can help me. Would you be able to do that?"

"Of course, buddy. Always happy to lend a dime if I can."

"All I need is a conversation."

"Okay, Mac. What you want to talk about?"

"Call me Alex. And I want to know all about what you do for a day job."

"Nothing much, Alex. Keep the peace. Try to stop people from hurting each other."

"That's what I heard. I admire guys like you who put their lives on the line every day for a handful of green."

"Thank you. What's this really about? I mean, Ezra, with all due respect, you didn't come down to this dive joint just to introduce me to a friend to blow smoke up my ass."

"Smart fella, isn't he, Ezra?"

"I told you, Alex, he's a sharp one."

"Sure did. Why don't we go somewhere more private to carry on this conversation...? Take your drink."

1910 ♦♦♦ **1920** ♦♦♦ 1930 ♦♦♦ 1940 ♦♦♦ 1950 ♦♦♦ 1960 ♦♦♦ 1970

19

FRANKIE DIDN'T APPEAR too worried as they meandered around the tables to reach Ezra's office. Once inside, Alex walked over and sat in Ezra's chair behind the desk, leaving the two others to seat themselves facing him.

"Ezra tells me he holds several of your markers and he wonders how you will make good on your debt."

"It's only a turn of a card away. I'm sure of that."

"I admire your faith in this uncertain world, Frankie, but sometimes self-belief is not enough. Do you have any collateral we can hold until the repayments are complete?"

"Collateral? I'm just a beat cop with a wife and kids. I ain't got nothing fancy like that."

Alex let those words hang in the air. He needed Frankie to think beyond his blind hope that he could double up his bets to get himself out of the deep hole he'd dug for himself. Besides, Alex already knew Frankie's apartment was rented, and he barely found enough dough for Mrs. Lando to buy groceries for the week.

The bright lights behind Frankie's eyes faded as he too realized today's meeting was more than a chat. Ezra had allowed him to amass the debt. At any point he could have stopped Frankie's line of credit, but he hadn't. Now, he was in hock to these serious men.

"Don't undersell yourself, Frankie. You don't have any collateral to offer me but you are still of value."

"Nice of you to say, but I don't see how."

"Ezra tells me you recently got a promotion. You're no longer walking the beat."

Frankie nodded but his expression showed no understanding.

"You're working at the Bureau of Prohibition nowadays. From what I hear, the pay's not much better than wearing a uniform."

"I get by."

"You need to do more than that, Frankie. Think of Eleanor and your kids. Don't they want a better life? Pretty clothes and somewhere safe to live."

"We live in a good neighborhood, Alex. Queens may not be fancy..."

"...but are they really safe there? That's what you must ask yourself."

Again, the implication of Alex's words slowly sank into Frankie's thick skull.

"What do you want from me?"

"The conversation we are having right now. Tell me more about what you do at the bureau."

THE FOLLOWING NIGHT, Alex and his men took a trip to Harlem. They had a bite to eat at the Club Deluxe and then went west until they met up with some of Massimo's guys on the corner of 145th and Riverside Drive. Two blocks north and the gang reached their destination: an unassuming warehouse with a pair of bored guards at the main entrance and nobody inside. Just as Frankie had described.

A truck pulled up on the opposite side of the street but the driver remained in the vehicle. One guard investigated this suspicious occurrence because he had nothing better to do and trucks rarely parked out this way in the middle of the night.

Alex watched as the guy approached from the passenger side and promptly vanished. His pal, still stood at the gate, had seen none of this because at the same moment, he was offering Massimo a light.

To thank him for his act of kindness, Massimo cracked the guy's skull as he turned away, with just enough force to knock him unconscious.

The instructions from Alex had been very clear—despite how you might feel about these guys, don't hurt them. We want the contents of the warehouse because it is our liquor they have seized, and we are also showing Uncle Sam not to get in the way of our business. And our enterprise is making money, not homicide.

The bonded warehouse contained over a hundred thousand dollars of booze, almost all of which had been taken from the Lower East Side and, even if it hadn't been, the hooch was now in Alex's hands. Before the break of dawn, enough trucks had driven uptown to ensure there was no alcohol inside the building apart from a small flask they had left in the locked room where they dumped the two guards.

Later that morning, Alex visited Arnold Rothstein to let him know in person about the recapture of his assets. Whereas almost every businessman had an office to conduct private meetings, the Big Bankroll chose a rear table at Lindy's Restaurant on Broadway between Forty-ninth and Fiftieth.

Amid the hustle and bustle of patrons eating cheesecake, pastries or even a full meal of *gefilte* fish and *latkes*, Rothstein held court, although there was never more than one other fella at his table. That way there were never any witnesses to anything that was said. Like Alex, he wrote nothing down. What Rothstein couldn't remember wasn't worth knowing.

"Thanks for your time, Alex. We shall ensure we show you some appreciation."

"Very kind, Arnold, but let's just make sure we take care of my guys."

"Don't be noble. It is a *mitzvah* for me to thank you. A blessing and you should not take it away from me."

HAVING DEVOTED THE morning to Arnold, Alex headed downtown to speak with Waxey; his life spent in the orbit of the Big Bankroll had been exhilarating. The man had ideas that spread beyond the here and now, but he was always focused on the next deal. His gambler's mind reassessed the risks of any venture each time some new piece of information came to light. Alex relished being in his company and not solely because everyone he worked with made a ton of money.

By the time his cab dropped him onto the corner of Bayard and Bowery, Alex was fired with excitement at the prospect of working with Arnold on his next project, whenever that might be. His heart shrank to the size of a nickel once Waxey briefed him on the next task for his boss.

"Let me get this straight; you want me to crack some heads in a *schmatta* factory?"

"There's been some unrest and we need some calm in there. You know how to handle union hotheads, which is why I'm asking you to intercede on my behalf."

"Why do you need me? Surely this is something one of my boys could take care of. My time is better spent elsewhere."

"For sure, but my niece will need careful management and I am relying on you."

"And she is the union convener, Waxey?"

"She is, so no rough stuff. Convince her to do the right thing for her workers but there should be no bruises, no scars. Lean on her only if you must and only as much as is absolutely necessary."

Waxey hadn't explained why his niece spent her days sewing for a living but Alex knew that even with that blood tie, Ezra could have been trusted with the task. Because he had been their gofer for so many years, they might have given him more authority, but Waxey and Ira had yet to show him the respect his new position commanded.

When he arrived at the factory—one of the many peppering the piers near the Williamsburg Bridge—Alex found Raymond Cooper Inc to be the same as any other warehouse in the block, with one exception. It was the only building that had strikers marching in front.

Alex sighed. It was always easier to get both sides to see reason before anyone did anything stupid like withdrawing their labor or sending in scab workers. Tempers would be frayed and emotions would be higher than Alex needed them to be.

"Can you tell me how to find Noga Spencer?"

The guy with the banner pointed at the far side of this huddle of twenty folk. Alex walked around the group rather than push through the crowd, his natural impulses restrained by the necessity to keep everything cool.

"Noga?"

"Yes, bud."

"I'm here to help your cause."

"Pick up a placard and join us. You work round here?"

"Not anymore. I meant to help you end the strike. I'm not one to stand on street corners complaining."

"Who sent you and what do you really want? Are you one of Cooper's men?"

"Not at all. Why are you striking?"

"Cooper is paying us a pittance and fails to look after the girls when they are too ill to work."

"So more pay and a day off to recuperate once in a while."

"Something like that."

"And Cooper thinks he pays you enough and doesn't see why someone can't spend six days a week in front of a sewing machine and live through the winter."

"Pretty much, bud. Who did you say you were with?"

"Just a concerned citizen. Which is more important to you, the extra money or the time off?"

"The gelt but we want both."

"Your sort always does, but you'll settle for less. And if Cooper won't give in to your demands?"

"Then we'll stay outside until he does."

"Is there scab labor inside?"

"Yeah…"

"So he has no need for you anymore. If you walked away from this place and didn't come back, Cooper would never even notice."

Noga stared straight at Alex for the longest time. Like she knew deep down he was right but didn't want to admit to him or herself that she'd led her people out of the promised land and onto the unforgiving streets of New York.

"How long have you been out here?"

"A week."

"And the scabs?"

"Second day."

"Let me have a word with Cooper."

Alex knocked on the door and was eventually let in. He waited in an anteroom until Cooper was prepared to receive his unexpected visitor.

"Thank you for seeing me without an appointment. As I said to your assistant, I'm hoping to help end this ridiculous strike."

"All the girls have to do is come back inside. One of them was sick, and I didn't complain while she was off for a week, but when she returned, she spent most of her time coughing her lungs up or in the bathroom. So I let her go. The next day, the rest of them refused to come in."

"What can I say, Raymond? I am not here to defend their actions but I would like to see this matter settled."

"You and me both."

"Quite. Is there anything you could offer them to bring them back in, no matter how empty the gesture?"

"I don't see why I should. I've got others doing their jobs right now. My plan was to get the police to clear the street tomorrow."

"In the past, the local law enforcement haven't much cared how they treat strikers during such operations. I wouldn't want anybody to be hurt."

Cooper looked at Alex while he stared directly through this upstart tailor. The cops would break heads if they had a chance and Noga was not to even suffer a bruise.

"Let the workers back in and I'll make sure your factory doesn't meet with any unexpected accident—like a fire suddenly sweeping through your premises tonight."

"Don't threaten me, mister. I already pay protection to stop those kinds of events from happening. You should have done your homework before trying to hustle me."

"Raymond, your protection money won't save you, because you need to make extra plans. I am asking you for some consideration, a personal favor if you will."

"You never gave me your name."

"Alex Cohen."

20

ALEX CAME UP with excuses to visit Arnold Rothstein from time to time. He made the Big Bankroll aware of his plans and sought his advice on matters. This was the first man Alex had met who he respected. Waxey was and remained a really great guy, but they understood each other too well and took each other for granted.

There was a tract of land immediately north of Alex's territory which looked ripe for picking so Alex asked Arnold for his thoughts.

"Gramercy is tempting, don't you think?"

"Are your eyes bigger than your stomach?"

"How so?"

"Who controls the park area now?"

"It's Italian."

"Don't be coy. Be serious in business always. If you don't know the answer to that question then don't start the conversation."

"My apologies, Arnold. We both know I am hemmed in north and west by Maranzano. From my perspective, north is easier to punch into than heading toward Mulberry and the heart of the Italian community."

"That much makes sense to me, but you might like to consider a different approach than brandishing your muscle."

Alex looked puzzled as brute force had got him to his current position. Before the war, he'd been known as the Slugger.

"Collaborate, my friend. When the pie is big enough, taking a share can still earn you more than owning all of a single cookie."

"I'm not too sure."

"Whatever you decide, you will need to discuss matters with Meyer Lansky. His interests and mine are closely aligned, and he does much more direct business with Maranzano than I do right now. If you are to succeed, you need his support. Let me make the introductions."

MEYER LANSKY WAS a stubby young man; what he lacked in height he made up for in girth, but Alex was no fool. Just because the guy appeared mildly comical—like a beach ball if you squinted— didn't mean you should treat him with anything but the utmost seriousness. The fella had Rothstein's ear and worked on a daily basis with Charlie Lucky. No one else in New York City could make that boast stick.

"Thanks for meeting with me, Mr. Lansky. You sure have a swanky apartment."

"You're welcome and thank you for your kind words. I hope you don't mind but I have no office. Those sorts of places attract undesirable kinds of people."

"I'm surprised to hear you allow panhandlers to get within fifty feet."

"They don't. I was referring to the cops and assassins. A gentleman should be able to conduct his business without worrying about who is coming through the door."

At that moment, a fella appeared in Lansky's living room, and walked over to whisper in his ear. Alex jumped out of his seat for a moment due to the unfortunate timing of Lansky's words. The near-silent conversation lasted only a minute then Alex was alone with Lansky again.

"Our mutual friend suggested I speak with you."

Alex explained his current situation in the Lower East Side and how he was looking to punch north provided he had appropriate support.

"And you are seeking my help?"

"Mr. Rothstein is on board if you are."

"I don't care either way and that is a statement of pure neutrality. I say this because I own no territory so your control of some blocks in Manhattan are immaterial to me. I mean you no offense."

"None taken."

Alex let that lie slip from his tongue because he understood that Lansky saw this as a business matter, so literally nothing for him was personal.

"My interest is piqued by any fresh opportunities you create by running that part of town. While Arnold was kind to send you my way, he knows there is someone else whose approval you need to seek: Charlie Lucky."

Alex's heart sank with those words. As much as Charlie had backed him since Prohibition made them all rich, Alex knew that Charlie preferred things the way they were. Change was bad for his business and right now there was a tension bubbling under the surface between Italian factions and Charlie wouldn't want anybody to rock the boat.

"So you're saying 'no' then."

"I'm saying 'not yet'. Charlie has other plans that need to be put in place before we do anything between the Lower East Side and Times Square. Your moment to shine will come—just not today."

ALEX RETURNED TO his office with his tail between his legs. No matter how much he wanted to push hard uptown, he would die trying without the support of Rothstein, Lansky and Charlie. The next best option before him was to make more money with what he already controlled.

"What I'm looking for," he explained to his crew, "is something we've not done before that'll earn us plenty. Don't give me an answer now—go away and come up with an idea. There's a two-thousand-dollar bonus to anyone with a suggestion we can turn into reality."

There had never been so many blank stares at the ground in the entire history of Manhattan.

"No rush. Give me any of your thoughts some time this week."

He wasn't expecting much from his men but he figured he'd give them a chance to come good. Meantime, Alex wandered the streets hoping a money-making scheme would pop into his head just by breathing in the same air as the johns who came to his bars and whorehouses.

The common problem with their flophouses was that the cops mapped exactly what they were and where they were. This entailed spending unnecessary amounts of cash on kickbacks just to keep the uniforms away.

Then there were the johns themselves. They always wanted to spend as little time in the joints as possible, which was good for the nafkas because they could move on to the next customer, but this was a nightmare for the owner. You spent your whole life desperately finding the next man to push through the front door.

When the nafka trade went well, the bars groaned in their emptiness like a stomach starved of bread. And the trouble with barflies was that their behavior would go downhill the more time they spent in the establishment. Even the arrival of the speakeasy did nothing to deal with the drunks. Alex introduced dance nights to many of his blind pigs and this meant a few more women showed up but takings were rarely up; they just didn't slump.

Alex continued musing on this dichotomy as he leaned against a wall and noticed he'd wandered over to the Forsyth Hotel. As his eyes focused on the building in front of him, he recalled his early days in the city and the number of times he'd watched Sarah's soft curves float up and down the main staircase.

His eyebrows raised and the flicker of an idea spread across his mind. They would create a modern version of the Forsyth as a speakeasy and whorehouse. The riffraff would not be allowed into the joints because they'd have gatekeepers on the door—that was normal for speakeasies. And the men who turned up could have a drink at a table, a show, and female companionship in equal measure.

Gaming tables in the back might even attract a different john. They could add those at a later date if they thought it would increase profit. The advantage of this idea was that Alex could choose his locations carefully and whichever street corner he chose, the owners would be sure to agree to sell to him. That much was certain.

21

AS MUCH AS Alex disliked giving handouts to cops, he knew cash was the oil that greased the machine. Once the new venues were running, the beat uniforms would only know the closed front doors, but that didn't mean there'd be no itchy palms before that point.

He sent a lad over to the Thirteenth Precinct station house on Clinton between First and Second Streets to request the company of Captain Mort Frye at his office. When the boy returned, he looked downcast.

"What happened?"

"Took me ages to find the fella and when I did, I told him exactly what you said. Then he clipped me round the ear and kicked my butt clear out the station."

"Something for you to learn about cops, son; unless you're dangling them by the ankles out of a twenty-story building, they'll show you no respect at all. Here's some shrapnel for your troubles."

He handed the kid a dollar because there's nothing worse than being publicly humiliated when you are ten years old. Besides, the boy had spunk to get inside the place and fight his way through to the big man himself.

This left the question of whether Frye had taken the message seriously. Alex remained behind his desk all morning and just before lunchtime, the squeak of leather could be discerned even before the office door creaked open and Frye stood surveying the scene.

Ezra and Massimo shuffled out with no word from Alex. No one wanted to stay in a room with a precinct captain.

"Sit down, Captain Frye, and I appreciate you traveling all this way to see me."

"I don't like being summoned, Cohen, especially not by your sort."

While he wasn't expecting a warm welcome, Alex rankled because he couldn't decide if Frye was objecting to him because of his business connections or lack of foreskin. The former was part of the job, the latter was prejudice and Alex had no time for that in his life. Whatever the reason, Alex told himself to keep calm because he wanted this jackass onside—else it would cost him in the long run.

"If my office is not to your liking, then I am more than happy for us to relocate to a place of your choosing."

"In an ideal world, you'd be in the precinct with handcuffs behind your back."

"We don't always get what we want, Captain Frye, but sometimes we can benefit from life's twists and turns. Sit down and let's talk... would you like a coffee?"

"If you are a legitimate businessman—and nothing I've heard about you indicates you are—then you wouldn't seek a private meeting with me."

"And if you were a legitimate police officer, you wouldn't be sitting here questioning my provenance."

"Well, I..."

"Your sort shouldn't take offense. I'm calling the situation as I see it. There's no need for either of us to get upset. I notice you have a taste for expensive shoes. I'd warrant they cost more than a month's pay, so please don't become indignant with me when I ask one of New York's finest to pay me a visit."

Frye glared at Alex until the fire ebbed from his eyes, while Alex enjoyed his drink.

"What would you like to talk about?"

"Soon I shall invest in local real estate and I'd like you to help me secure my investments."

"That's what the police are here to do."

"I figured. During the acquisition and preparation phases, I'd like your lads to keep a watchful eye on the properties."

"That can be arranged..."

"And after that I want to be left alone."

"Also within my reach."

"Pleased to hear it. For the first piece, I will make a donation to the Police Benevolent Fund and give you the money to pass on to the proper authorities."

"Thank you for your contribution and happy to oblige."

"And with the second part, let me be clear about what I want. There should be no unpleasant interference from any criminal element..."

A smile trickled from the corner of Frye's mouth but he understood that Alex didn't want the local kids robbing from him.

"...and your officers shouldn't come round snooping for a handout either. If you and I take care of business, then I need not pay anybody else."

"That can also be arranged and you have my personal guarantee that none of them boys will bother your people."

"Good news. Again I will use you as a conduit to the Police Benevolent Fund, assuming that is acceptable to you."

"Mighty swell, Mr. Cohen."

"Call me Alex; Mr. Cohen sounds like you're talking to my father."

NOVEMBER 1922

22

THANKS TO THE payoffs to Frye, all the new speakeasy brothels opened on schedule with a minimum of fuss and little or no interference from the cops. Alex marveled at how you could get anything that you wanted in this beloved country, provided you paid for it.

On some occasions Ezra would hand over the gelt and sometimes Alex would be the one to make others' dreams come true.

Voting in America had always been a lynchpin of the New World's democratic principles and the situation in New York reflected this. Manhattan naturally found its own way to express the power of the people with Tammany Hall, which exerted a stranglehold on election results.

Alex's new role on the Lower East Side meant there were certain duties to perform on the day of the state elections, which dated back at least a century to the time when the Democratic Party first interfered directly in the results of the people's vote.

"This is the deal." Alex issued his final orders in his office before the polling booths opened.

"We have identified which wards need our special attention. Make sure you have a copy of the list before you leave."

Heads nodded, but no one moved because they could tell the briefing was not over.

"We may come across individuals who do not take kindly to our approach in dishing out democracy. They are entitled to their opinion, but that does not mean they should express their views in public. Feel free to discourage them using any appropriate means necessary. They must all still be breathing when you leave them— with no exceptions. The only accidents I want to hear about are unintended stuffing of other ballot boxes. Is that clear?"

Tammany Hall had been the center of Democratic Party influence in New York for as long as people could remember and during that time, men like Tammany's boss Charles Murphy paid immigrants like Alex Cohen to fix election results. There was no other explanation of how the Democrats maintained their stranglehold on power for so long.

Alex didn't care much for politics or politicians. These were the people who had taken the country into the Great War and had allowed soldiers to die in the trenches over there. But, despite his dislike for those involved in electioneering, Alex's desire to acquire wealth and power meant he was more than prepared to do business with Murphy and his ilk.

Besides, he might think they were scum, but politicians had influence which he knew was a useful commodity and his newfound friends, Arnold and Meyer, recognized the importance of keeping these fellows onside. It was good for business—and Alex sure understood that.

DECEMBER 1922

23

THE END OF 1922 was a blessing and a curse. Overall, it had been a good year for Alex, his men and his business associates, although he was concerned that the hard-fought success he'd achieved would get swept away. This reflected Alex's lack of security and confidence as opposed to any identifiable threat.

"You fret too much."

"Sure, Arnold, but…"

"But, nothing. Once you've played your hand, the only thing left to do is to see how the other cards land. It is too late to worry at that point and you must accept your lot. You cannot change the past, only shape the future."

Rothstein was right and Alex knew; he just wasn't satisfied until he picked at the scab and made it bleed. He was grateful for the invitation from Arnold to join him and his wife for a New Year's Eve celebration at the Waldorf Astoria Hotel on Fifth Avenue and Thirty-third.

While he might have worried he was punching above his weight, Alex accepted his seat at the table almost before the offer had been uttered. How could he refuse such a kind invitation from the Big Bankroll?

The evening began with champagne cocktails in Arnold's suite. Alex and Sarah were introduced to Lansky and his wife, Benny Siegel and a brunette, and Charlie Lucky with his wife. Waxey and

Ira were nowhere to be seen and Alex was confused for a moment. He'd assumed he would have been invited to a large party, not to an intimate gathering of the Big Bankroll's close business partners.

Sarah kept a tight grip on his hand and only after she'd downed the second glass of bubbly did she relax enough to allow their palms to separate. "I really don't feel like I should be here," she whispered, and Alex knew how she felt.

Once the cocktails were consumed, the party moved downstairs into the Grand Hall where their table was waiting. To book a spot inside that room on that night meant you were either rich beyond most people's dreams or incredibly powerful—or both. Both Alex and Sarah did their best to use the right silverware, and the waiters acted polite but haughty.

At some point when Alex was wrestling the bones of a salmon out of its flesh, Charles Murphy wandered by to pay his respects to Rothstein and stop for a conversation with Alex. He eyed Sarah almost the entire time he spoke—she had lost none of her allure in the five years since Alex first glimpsed her ankle.

"We appreciate all your efforts last month, Alex... and who is this ravishing creature?"

"Charles, let me introduce my wife, Sarah."

"Charmed, dear lady."

"Likewise, I'm sure."

"You and your husband must visit some time. We'd love to have you over for tea."

"That'd be lovely. Why don't I leave you men to make all the arrangements?"

Sarah might have believed she was a fish out of water, but she was familiar enough with the men to recognize trouble when she saw it. You didn't need to be a follower of politics to sense that Murphy's intentions would not be honorable. She knew a john when one walked up to her.

The rest of the meal passed without incident and when everyone in the room had finished eating, the orchestra stopped playing and were replaced by a jazz band. Sarah grabbed Alex by the hand and, not for the first time, she dragged him onto the dance floor. Within minutes they were joined by twenty or more couples until the place was heaving. She leaned into Alex and stretched up so her lips were nestling by his right ear.

"I'm glad we came. Are you having fun, because I am. I thought these people would be too snooty but Arnold and Meyer are cool guys."

"They sure are, hon'. Benny's okay too but he always has a different twist on his arm, so that can be kinda awkward. The guy can't settle down."

"You socialize with Benny often?"

"Not really, but he's the only one of us who doesn't have a steady."

At midnight, a thousand balloons descended from the ballroom ceiling and Alex shook hands with Arnold, Meyer and Charlie Lucky. Then he turned to kiss and hug Sarah.

"We've made it, honey. This is the life, don't ya think?"

"Sure do. Just remember, it's not the money but who you are that makes me love you though."

Alex looked at her quizzically but before she could explain, they were separated by the tide of revelers wishing everybody and anything a Happy New Year. The dancing continued and everyone carried on drinking their coffees laced with liquor until the small hours.

How did a respectable establishment get away with serving high-grade alcoholic beverages? Because there were enough judges in the room to throw out any court case and the providers of the booze were in the joint too.

By six am, the party was fading, and they called it quits. Arnold, Meyer and their spouses returned to Rothstein's suite—Benny and his squeeze had slunk away several hours earlier. This left Alex and Sarah to walk through reception and stand to wait for a taxi.

Despite the early time of day, a yellow cab swung by within seconds and halted in front of the hotel. Alex let Sarah get in first and she shimmied over the back seat to make room for her husband.

As Alex bent down to join her, a bullet zinged past, missing his head by inches. If he'd been standing upright then his brains would have been mixing with the white walls of the entrance.

Out of sheer instinct, he slammed the cab door shut and hit the dirt. The vehicle sped away with Sarah screaming as the driver exited the area at high velocity. This left Alex exposed although he had no clue where the assailant was located. He scurried to the revolving doors and rolled back inside. Uniformed cops appeared less than a minute later but, even if he'd wanted to help, Alex could tell them *gornisht*. When he finally made it home an hour later, he checked on the kids who were already awake and then lay on the bed and fell asleep within seconds.

24

IMAGES AND SOUNDS appeared to Alex from the depths of his subconscious while he slept. An alleyway in the mist. One stocky figure shuffled into view. Bruises and blood around his head and neck. Alex recognized the guy despite his disfigured features.

"Sammy?"

"Who else do you think it could be?"

"How are you after all this time?"

"I'm surprised you care... I'm not too bad under the circumstances."

"Huh?"

"How are you and how is Sarah?"

"Someone shot at us earlier today and I haven't seen her since then. You seen her passing by?"

"No, not that I noticed, but no one wanders into this alley. I was surprised to see you, to be honest."

Alex looked at his surroundings and realized where he was. This was where he'd first met Sammy when he arrived in town and the same place where he'd nearly clubbed his friend to death three years later. He turned his attention back to Sammy; more bruises had appeared around his eyes and his neck was discolored.

"Are you certain you are okay?"

"Don't worry about me. Focus on Sarah. You said you hadn't seen her."

"Not since the shooting."

"You might want to think about how you treat her."

"What do you mean?"

"You allowed someone to fire a bullet within a foot of her head. That's not exactly protecting her from harm. Does she deserve that?"

Alex looked down to his feet as his cheeks heated. He shoved his hands into his pants pockets.

"I do my best to provide for her. A roof over her head; I buy her pretty things. She tells me I'm a good provider."

"But you didn't take care of her today. She nearly died by your side."

"Have you seen her? She ran off in a cab and I haven't seen her since."

"She'll be back eventually. You need to do a better job of keeping her safe."

"Yes, I intend to."

"I hope those aren't empty words—you made me many promises and didn't keep them. Can she trust you?"

"Of course."

"If you want her to continue to trust you, then you must tread carefully."

"What do you mean?"

"The life you lead; the people you meet. This criminal world you inhabit is filled with opportunities to do the right thing and the ever-present possibility of making poor decisions."

"I don't understand what you're saying."

"Alex, you run prostitutes the length of Manhattan. Are you telling me you've never considered sampling the merchandise?"

Sammy's statement was met with a blank expression.

"Not once. There's only ever been one nafka I slept with and that was Sarah. At that time, she wasn't one of my girls."

"How noble, Alex. But you need to make sure you do the right thing by her."

"We are married, Sammy, and she has given me two boys."

"Just remain on a straight and righteous path or you will lose that woman. All the shiny expensive jewelry in the world won't keep her by your side if you veer from the one true road."

The mist thickened, and it seemed to Alex that Sammy was floating away. Then in an instant he was back, inches from Alex's bulbous nose.

"And one more comment before I must leave. How much longer will you stay with Waxey? When will you fly away?"

"Waxey saved me."

"Are you duty bound to sit by his feet until the day he dies?"

"That's not what I mean. I owe him some allegiance but I'm not shackled to him in the way you are implying."

"The secret to a successful career is knowing when it's time to go."

"And is that what you think I should do?"

"My opinions don't count. Do you think there is more to learn from Waxey?"

"He saved my life," Alex mumbled under his breath to emphasize how little he believed his own words.

"Eventually that debt will be paid and then you must decide whether Charlie Lucky or Lansky will make a more interesting business partner."

"Or Arnold. I could learn so much from that man."

"Before you make your selection, you'd need to leave Waxey and find out which of those gents would be prepared to have you come along for the ride."

"I'm happy where I am."

"Don't lie to me, Alex Cohen. You've found so many ways to create an excuse to see Rothstein and you even had a secret meeting with Lansky. So don't pretend to be all innocent with me."

"How d'you know about that?"

"I know everything you know. And more besides. Who's it going to be? Charlie Luciano or Meyer Lansky?"

"Arnold Rothstein?"

"You'd like to be him, wouldn't you? But he's too refined a gentleman and you are too much of a street fighter. Know thyself, Alex."

The mist grew thicker again until Alex was forced to close his eyes to prevent them from stinging. He clenched them tight for over a minute and when he opened them again, he found himself on top of his bed with all his clothes on. Sarah lay next to him asleep. He slipped off his pants and shoes and clambered under the covers without waking her. Alex leaned in to smell the perfume of Sarah's body and drifted back into unconsciousness with the comfort of knowing she was safe and sound, despite her snoring.

JANUARY 1923

25

TWO DAYS LATER and the dust had settled on the attack. Waxey appeared unconcerned. "It's the life we lead," was his comment, but he did not pass a thought on how Sarah might feel. This was not the world she was living in. Not at all.

From what Alex could see, she was shaken but not frightened. While she understood the hit was meant for him, she remained angry, whereas he got that this was business and nothing personal.

In part driven by Waxey's indifference and partly in response to his dream, Alex spent his time with Arnold. The man had shown real sympathy, even offering the Cohens the opportunity to remain at the Waldorf as his guests for a few days.

"That's very kind of you and much appreciated, but we are going to stay put. Sarah doesn't want the kids' lives to be disrupted and my best men surround the place day and night."

"I understand. If you change your mind, then you just say."

"What I would like to do is chat with whoever squeezed the trigger."

Lansky sat back on a couch, comfortable in the surroundings of Arnold's hotel suite. Charlie Lucky had joined them and Alex was pleased to be in their company. He was punching well above his weight.

"We are making discreet enquiries on your behalf. This was not a random act; some coward attacked you in front of your wife while you were attending my party."

Charlie sat next to Lansky and nodded; they had grown up together and continued to work closely together. The Italian sipped his coffee before passing comment.

"We will find the dog who did this and make an example of him, for sure, but right now let's return to business. We need to talk more about our supply lines…"

A WEEK LATER, Alex received a phone call in his office.

"Charlie here."

"How are you?"

"All good. I'll be quick. The fella you're looking for is ready for a conversation with you."

"Which guy?"

"The one who tried to kill you."

Alex fell silent for three, maybe four, seconds.

"Hello. Are you still there?"

"Yes, I was thinking."

"My men are holding him until you arrive but take your time because this fella ain't goin' nowhere."

"Thank you. I owe you one."

"Nah. We live together, we fight together…"

"But we die alone, I know."

"Not for a very long while unless some chump tries to whack you when you're leaving a party: scum."

The phone went dead and Alex sat there, letting the buzz of the office engulf him. Then he blinked, swigged his coffee until the mug was empty and turned to Ezra.

"Don't wait up. I may be gone some time."

"Let me go with you."

"No need. Charlie's found my unknown assailant."

Despite Alex's protestations, Ezra drove him over to the hideout and strode inside the westside warehouse. The cavernous space at the heart of the building contained a table, a few chairs, and five men, one of whom was tied to a chair.

As they walked nearer to the huddle, Alex saw the fellas standing around doing nothing in particular. The guy with the ropes round his wrists was bruised about the face and had two small pools of blood by his shoes. Luciano's guys had been professional throughout the encounter.

When he got within twenty feet of the group, the men stood straight like they knew who he was, even though Alex didn't recognize any of this crew.

"Anyone know the name of this *farbissener momzer?*"

"He's a neighborhood kid. A few of us have seen him around, but nobody knows the little *schmendrick.*"

Alex nodded and turned his attention to the boy. There was a gag in his mouth and Alex heard every inhalation and exhalation clear as day. After he approached, the breathing got more frequent and louder.

"Let's get these straps off your head, so we can talk."

He bent over the guy and undid the knot so the binding loosened and fell away from the boy's face. He then spat out a mouthful of muslin which had been forced past his lips earlier in the day. Alex looked round until Ezra supplied a chair which he placed opposite the lad.

"Before we start, I want you to listen carefully to what I have to say to you. Can you do that for me?"

"Yes, but this is a terrible mistake."

Alex put a solitary finger across his lips.

"We will talk about any mistakes in a minute. First, what is your name?"

"I'm scared that if I tell you, then you will harm my family."

"You have nothing to fear as I intend your kin no ill will. What is your name?"

"Savino Raneri."

"Why did you try to kill me and my wife?"

"I never aimed at her. Did she get hurt?"

"Bit late to worry about that now. No, she did not but you need to explain to me why you hid in the bushes and fired a shot at me."

The boy stopped talking and licked his lips. Alex indicated for one of the men to bring some water over. A few sips later and Alex repeated his question. Nada.

"Understand this. Either you answer my questions and you die an easy death, or refuse and these fellas will take their sweet time as they make you experience pain you can only imagine from your darkest nightmares. This is the only choice left."

Alex stared at those young eyes as they filled with fear, but no hate. There was nothing personal in the attack.

"This is my guess. You decided you wanted to skip working your way up and thought that whacking me would win you some friends in high places."

The boy's expression morphed from incredulity to panic to acceptance.

"Who do you work for, little man?"

The kid looked up but said nothing.

"I admire your chutzpah but you make terrible choices."

Alex stood up and nodded to Ezra. The boy's screams pierced Alex's ears until the gag was replaced. The next day, his corpse could be seen floating down the Hudson. He took four long hours to die and his body was a mess of bruises, cigarette burns, and cuts from various blades.

BOOZE IS A peculiar commodity; sometimes people are thirsty and other times not. January was one of those months when every bottle that arrived in Alex's warehouses shipped out the same day. Manhattan became a desiccated husk and Alex seized the opportunity as it presented itself.

He hightailed it over to Lindy's Restaurant and waited in line—not for a seat; that was easy to get—but for the table at the back of the establishment to be occupied by only one man: Arnold. When his turn arrived, Alex stepped forward with his coffee in hand and sat down next to Rothstein so neither would need to raise their voice much above a whisper.

"Thanks for seeing me."

"You didn't need to be here, Alex. We could have had a meeting in my suite."

"I understand, but I wanted you to know that I am not seeking any special favors, just a fair hearing."

"Talk to me."

As Alex inhaled, a waitress came over and delivered a large piece of cheesecake, forcing him to wait before pitching Rothstein.

"I'm moving every ounce of alcohol I can lay my hands on and it isn't enough. I need more territory to expand my storage capacity and to increase the number of locations to sell product. In short, I want to head north and reach out as far as Times Square eventually."

"Good to see a young man with fire in his belly and ambition coursing through his veins."

"And I'll need your support, Arnold, to do this. It'll cost hard gelt and your political protection. The Italians will not be impressed if I stomp over their territory."

"You are right to come to me again and I appreciate the respect you are showing me. Before I can decide whether to offer you the support you seek, I must ask you to do me a small favor."

"Name it."

"I'd like you to take a trip to Windsor for me."

26

THE TRIP TO Canada went smoothly but when Alex arrived in Windsor, the streets felt different to his last visit. The sidewalks were deserted—not just sparse but completely vacant—no one was out and about.

By the time he'd made his way to Arnold's contact on the far side of town on Dougall Avenue, Alex wondered whether the Spanish flu had descended on the inhabitants of this place. Its sole value to anyone beyond its civic border was its location so close to the US that you'd be forgiven for thinking you were still in America.

A rat-a-tat-tat on the door and a stranger let him in without even checking his credentials. He wasn't impressed with this lapse in security but bit his lip and followed the fella into an office.

"Wanna drink?"

"Coffee would be good."

A nod and the guy left, only to return three minutes later with a cup and a friend who introduced himself as Stefano Perisi, a thick mop of black hair upon his head.

"Thank you for coming, Mr. Cohen. We are living in troubling times."

"With no one guarding your front door, I'm not surprised you are troubled."

"Huh? We knew you were showing up and no one else would have turned up at this hour apart from you. Baggi holds the entire town in his clenched fist. Didn't you notice how few people were on the streets? The ordinary citizens are too scared to come out of their homes. No local would have knocked on our door out of the blue. So it had to be you."

"Who is this Baggi?"

"Fabiana Baggi is backed by friends from the East Coast. Nobody knows who but they have muscle and money. In only a handful of weeks, they've taken control of every place you can cross the river by boat. And, as you know, Windsor needs its supply lines, or it is nothing. Once they did that, all they needed to finish the job was to hit our warehouses. Within a week, they had the liquor, the boats, the trucks. Everything. And we were left holding our dicks."

"Stefano, Baggi might have borrowed this hick town for two weeks, but I am here to convince him to return what is not his."

"Not being funny, but good luck. Baggi's brought an army with him and they take no prisoners. You are with them or dead."

"I shall have a word with Fabiana Baggi and see if we can reach a businesslike arrangement."

STEFANO GAVE DIRECTIONS to Baggi's headquarters and offered to send one of his men to accompany Alex but he refused. There was no point putting another life in jeopardy, he'd said. Truth was that Alex didn't want to be associated with the local hoods any way at all. He wanted Baggi to see him in a different light.

Before he'd opened the door of his car, he felt a thousand gun barrels aimed at his head, so he eased himself out of the vehicle, careful to keep his hands visible at all times and to adopt a casual air as he sauntered to the building.

The clunk of bolts being unlocked met him as he approached until a voice called out from the inky blackness of the interior for him to stop in his tracks and assume the position. Alex halted and raised his hands above his head, thinking the phrase the guy had used made him sound like a cop.

The fella stepped out of the shadows, frisked him, and led him inside with the cold steel of his shotgun square between Alex's shoulder blades. This was just another tumbledown bar in a part of town which couldn't remember it had ever seen better days. He was pushed into a side room and waited ten long minutes before anybody returned. Even with no introduction, he sensed the guy before him was Baggi. The two stared at each other until Baggi broke the silence.

"What do you want?"

"A conversation with you."

"Baggi is listening."

"I represent some business interests from back east who had been using Windsor for a profitable enterprise until you arrived and prevented us from carrying out our commercial activities."

"Why should Baggi care about this?"

"These interests would like to reach an accommodation with you so that we may continue to ply our trade and you may still do... whatever you do here."

"Make money. Baggi is here to look after his friends' business interests."

"We need not be in conflict. We all want a clean supply of liquor from Windsor through to Manhattan and can work together to protect this route from outside interference."

"Baggi needs no help from a Jew."

Alex ground his molars but knew better than to respond with fist-thumping violence, his first impulse.

"Until now, the Sugar House Gang in Detroit has been under strict instruction not to attack your trucks once they've crossed the Detroit River because we wanted to give you the opportunity to work with us."

"Baggi is not concerned about a handful of bad-blood Jews. You are not offering Baggi anything of interest."

"Then I shall take my leave and remind you that I came here today with open arms and a desire to negotiate a deal."

Baggi stood up from his chair and let one of his goons march Alex off the premises. As he crossed the threshold, Alex turned his head around and smiled. Baggi had followed him out. Despite the Italian's bold words, he was worried, otherwise he'd have returned to whatever he'd been doing before Alex had appeared from nowhere.

Alex jumped back into his car and traveled at a sensible pace to his hotel—the joint had been warned of his impending arrival the previous day. Sure enough, John Smith signed into his room and called down for service as soon as the bellboy had pocketed his quarters and left.

Then Alex took off his shoes and stretched his toes before he picked up the handset by the bed and asked the operator to place a call to New York. A brief conversation and everything was sorted, so he savored every mouthful of his steak, knowing there was nothing more for him to do that night.

Despite himself, Alex slept until seven but made sure he ate a full breakfast even though there were no bagels or blintzes. By nine he was sat in his car and a black suit approached him, hat brim positioned to hide his eyes.

"Good to see you, Massimo."

"Likewise, boss. Ezra and the crew are ready and waiting."

"Did you bring everything I asked?"

"Of course. We're looking forward to this party."

"Hop in and you can direct me to the fellas."

ONE HOUR LATER, Alex had issued instructions to the twenty men who had driven from New York on his command. A similar number had positioned themselves outside the warehouses which were crammed full of Rothstein-funded whiskey. They were to do nothing unless anybody tried to leave and then their orders were simple: kill anyone who moved. The horde with Alex were to wait until he gave the word.

"How can we be sure that Baggi is inside?"

"He's locked this town down tight and hasn't bothered to protect his place properly otherwise we wouldn't be talking right now. So, he's happy in his flophouse with all his guys on the inside."

Ezra smiled at his boss's cold logic and understanding of how his enemies thought.

"Let's show this Italian what Jews are capable of."

Ezra hustled off to speak to his men and a minute later, four metal projectiles flew toward the door and windows of Baggi's headquarters. As soon as the first one landed, immediately by the entrance, a blinding flash and ear-splitting roar erupted as if from nowhere. Then another, then a third swiftly followed by the fourth.

Dirt and debris flew into the air, some blasted into the nearby windows causing glass to shatter and implode, some hurtled up and cascaded on parked cars and smashed onto the ground. Alex saw the craters formed by the grenades and flashed back to France. Limbs strewn next to the bodies of his fallen comrades, faces skewed in distorted death stares.

Machine guns punctured his reverie and his men picked out Baggi's people one by one. Some made the mistake of fleeing the scene and they were the first to die. Over the course of the next five minutes, Alex's crew shot and killed every man who appeared at any window or door of the building. Then there was silence.

Alex listened to the wind and indicated for his men to do nothing. A hand gesture to Massimo and three guys scurried across the street and stood either side of what had been the main entrance. They popped their heads inside and another volley of gunfire followed.

More gesticulation and Alex ran over with ten men; the rest held back in case of further trouble. Alex looked around at the rubble and blood, trying to spot Baggi among the dead bodies. No joy.

He signaled two fellas to hop upstairs. One burst of gunfire and twenty seconds later, both returned. Time to check out the room he'd visited the previous day. Alex pushed the side door open and prepared for a dramatic response, but nothing. Along the corridor and he turned a handle to see what would happen. Zilch.

He kicked the door, and it flung wide to reveal the same furniture as before but no Baggi. At least, he wasn't visible but Alex could hear deep breathing instead. He pulled out a revolver and pointed it at a desk. The sound seemed to come directly from it. Sure enough, Alex found a man's ass protruding from under the oak.

"Get up, Baggi."

A whimper and the man shuffled out and rose to his full height, hands on his head. Alex edged forward and moved sufficiently close to push the barrel of his gun past Baggi's teeth and into his mouth.

The Italian mumbled something but none of his words could be understood because of the metal by his tongue. Alex didn't care precisely what was said because he could guess the general gist.

He shook his head and squeezed the trigger. Baggi wouldn't be getting an open casket funeral.

27

UPON HIS RETURN to the Big Apple, Alex had swung by Lindy's to report to Arnold. This time he didn't wait and headed straight to the front of the line to whisper the good news.

"Windsor is back under our control. I left some of my guys there in case there is any further trouble but that won't come from the Canadian end."

"Excellent. My friends north of your territory have agreed not to send any more of their associates over the border."

"We were fighting Maranzano's men?"

"Yes. Don't look at me like that with your puppy dog eyes and hurt expression. This is business. Occasionally I reach commercial arrangements with people you would prefer dead. That is the way of the world and nothing more. If you can't make peace with that stone-cold fact then you and I can no longer work together. That would be a shame because I think you could go far and we might both enjoy your success..."

"Because I'll need funding to get there?"

"Boychick, one day you'll be a *gantse mensch* at this rate. Of course I'll be there to prime the pump. We don't work as hard as this for the benefit of our health. Not me, for sure."

"Before I went off to fight in the war, I just wanted to survive. When I came back, I vowed I must never be in that situation again and money will protect me from returning to the gutter."

"Until it is our time to meet our maker."

Arnold fake-spat three times to ward off evil spirits and Alex didn't even blink, it was such a common occurrence among his people.

"Despite their assurances to you, when my men leave Windsor what'd stop Maranzano from moving back in?"

"Alex, they gave their word but I agree that this might not be enough."

"Although I wouldn't want to keep Ezra or Massimo stationed there, I could maintain a presence for a while."

"That would be helpful. The recent crisis has shown us we need to protect our assets more carefully. Would you be willing to run the Windsor end of the operation?"

"Sure."

"Then you should receive a percentage of the proceeds all my friends generate by you delivering them safe passage. Ten percent seems fair. Is that acceptable to you?"

"Of course. A very reasonable share, but I want you to know that my two best fellas will move back home soon."

"That is your business, not mine. All you must do is keep Windsor open for us. Who achieves that goal is down to you."

ONE DAY'S WORK had netted Alex a small fortune—not just today but far into the future. He understood that there was more to the deal than the removal of Fabiana Baggi and a grenade attack. That was the final piece of the jigsaw which had secured the offer but it meant he'd spent enough time in the presence of Arnold, Meyer and Charlie to gain their trust.

With the warm glow of pride ringing across his cheeks, Alex hurried home to Sarah to tell her the good news. He also needed to pack a bag and return to Windsor to put a more permanent solution in place than having Massimo and Ezra holed up in a fleapit hotel.

He took a train to Detroit and paid a visit to Abe Bernstein and the Sugar House gang. They sat in a private room at the back of a blind pig under Abe's control.

"Thank you for seeing me at short notice."

"Always good to see a friendly face. Word on the street tells me you were the other side of the river earlier this week."

"I'm glad your informers are earning their money. Yes, I had a little business to attend to, but that's all resolved."

"So I hear. Congratulations. We benefitted from that momzer's removal."

"His absence has certainly helped the flow of liquor to New York and our mutual friend sends his regards."

"Tell Arnold he should pop over here himself. I know of at least a dozen players who would chop off their mother's right arms to sit at the same green baize as the Big Bankroll."

"I'll tell him, but I make no promises."

They jawed over their previous encounter and Abe remarked on Alex's rise within the ranks. What the man didn't mention was how his position had improved too. When they'd last met, Abe and his brothers had taken control of most illegal activities in Detroit. Now thanks to Prohibition and the accidental location of Detroit so close to the Detroit River, no liquor survived the journey to Ohio without prior approval of the Sugar House gang.

"Alex, while it is truly wonderful to see you, were you doing anything more than merely passing through?"

"Ha ha. I respect you too much to pretend. I came here to discuss some business."

"Here we are. Speak."

"We both know the supply line from Manhattan requires Windsor to be under our wing and for you to extend safe passage to our transport. And you have always been kind enough to deliver that to us."

"For a price, Alex."

"I understand, Abe. You and Arnold have an agreement which both sides honor. But I'd like to suggest a supplementary arrangement on top of the existing deal."

"I'm listening. What do you have in mind?"

"Until now, if our trucks arrived in Detroit, you let them through. Our recent difficulty with Baggi has left me running Windsor with

Arnold's backing. So what I'd like us to agree is that if an issue arises in Canada then you'll sail over and assist."

"And for risking my men's lives when you are in trouble…?"

"I shall split my earnings with you fifty-fifty. That's five percent of the total revenues from real whiskey coming into New York."

"Alex, I am happy to help as our interests are mutually aligned in the success of the bootlegging operation. And while I admire your offer, I must refuse."

"But…"

"Hear me out. Your split is too generous. If I take your terms then in a year or two, you will resent the amount I get. We both realize that most of the time the Sugar House shall receive money for virtually nothing. Eventually, you will decide there is too much green heading our way and do something about it. Blood will be shed and one of us will be dead. I like you too much to want to kill you, so why don't I only accept two percent and then the problem won't arise."

"That is incredibly generous. I feel as though my offer was cheap and foolish."

"Not at all. I prefer business partners who are breathing and we will both make a large amount of money out of this venture no matter how we share out the proceeds."

28

A FIRM HANDSHAKE with Abe and the deal was secured. Alex then popped over the border to discuss his plans with Ezra and Massimo. The former stayed in Windsor while Massimo found a suitable permanent replacement. No sooner had Alex dropped into his chair in the office when a call came through from Charlie Lucky and he was back on his feet and out the door.

"Transportation. That's my problem, Alex."

Charlie and Alex stood in a warehouse near Pier 57 at the outer reaches of Fifth Street. The difficulty was in front of their eyes. Alex knew this prime location was usually full to the brim with people and contraband but today there were just the two of them and their echoes.

"I can probably get you five to ten trucks within the next day, Charlie, and more if I have longer."

"I'd appreciate that, but it's not my immediate concern."

"Don't take this the wrong way but why is a man like you coming to a guy like me for a handful of vehicles?"

"Never undersell yourself, Alex. The reason we are having this conversation is that last week the cops were all over me like a rash and I've got a shipment approaching our shores that needs a safe home with someone I can trust."

"You require boats, not trucks. When will the goods arrive?"

"Day after tomorrow, so you don't have much time to prepare."

"How safe a haven do you need, Charlie?"

"The twenty-pound shipment contains uncut opium."

Alex whistled, appreciating the audacity of Charlie's plan. A quick calculation off the top of his head showed there would be nearly one hundred pounds of heroin hitting the street.

"That's quite a party."

"The cops know the shipment is on its way and want to get their grubby hands on it, but I need you to find a secure location away from prying eyes where we can stash the brown powder until I offload it."

"I've got some ideas for storage and after a couple of phone calls, the boats won't be a problem either. The advantage to running booze from every direction into Manhattan is that there's always someone who will lend me a hand."

"Good news. Arnold thought you'd be the perfect man for the job."

Another discussion over money and a firm handshake. Now Alex was getting a piece of both the booze and the heroin action. As they left the empty warehouse together, he had every right to smile.

THE FRENETIC PACE of his life meant Alex hardly saw Sarah and his boys the following few weeks. His next port of call was Florida. While many might head south for the winter, Alex was arriving in March but he still appreciated the warmth compared to home.

Arnold had asked him to take the trip because he had a need for a combination of muscle and management. There was a financial institution where a local gang wanted to make an unexpected withdrawal. The First Bank of Florida was based in Miami but its branch in Boca Rotan was of greater interest.

While the area was filling up with members of New York and Chicago's criminal elements, there was still a large amount of old money that screamed to be liberated from the clutches of the Florida banking system.

Pete and Frank Bunyan had made overtures to Arnold who had shown an interest in financing the deal and handling the tricky job of laundering the ill-gotten gains. The robbery itself required a small group of tough guys to hit the joint with an almighty bang and to make good their escape before anyone noticed the money had left the building.

The brothers had secured a local driver for the getaway and Alex was there for crowd control. He would also monitor Arnold's investment, although the Bunyan boys didn't realize quite how close he was to Rothstein and made the mistake of thinking of him as just New York muscle.

"Are we clear about everything?"

The four erstwhile robbers sat at a table in a gambling den owned by Pete. Pete had run through the plan twice to make sure everyone knew what to do.

"Apart from the security guard, are we expecting anyone to be packing any heat?"

"There's no one else who we know has a gun on them, Alex. How Joe Public responds when we enter the joint is another thing altogether."

"For sure. Nothing personal but the way you describe it, this job is like taking candy from a baby, but I've been sent halfway across the country so something must make the task harder."

"It's what we're stealing. Gold bullion. We are not to touch any cash or jewelry. Only the gold in the safe. Mr. Rothstein was very clear that we are authorized to steal the yellow bars and nothing else."

Alex raised an eyebrow and he solemnly nodded his head to acknowledge Arnold's intentions. Pete explained how they'd handle the precious metal.

THE NEXT DAY, three men wearing scarves over their mouths and noses stormed into the First Bank of Florida, one toting an automatic machine gun and the other two sporting revolvers.

Pete shoved his pistol into the security guard's stomach and he raised his hands. Having removed the guy's pistol from its holster, Pete slammed the butt of his own revolver against the officer's temple and the uniform slumped down. Meanwhile, Frank and Alex scooted across the main area and over to the tellers.

Alex leaped on top of the counter to get a better view of all the citizens and made sure he brandished his weapon for everybody to see.

"Everyone on the ground, face down."

Within fifteen long seconds, the four men and three women had complied with Pete's instruction. The bank staff had hit the deck immediately because they knew that heroes die in robberies and besides, the bank was insured. Now the Bunyans could get to work.

Pete and Frank headed over the counter and scuttled to the safe leaving Alex to keep control of the johns. Two of the women whimpered, but from his vantage point, Alex could see all the customers and staff were frozen against the marble floor.

All except one. The guard had roused himself and Alex noticed the man was moving along the ground, slowly shuffling toward the main entrance. Alex couldn't tell if the uniform was planning on making a break for the door or if he wanted to get to his stool. The answer came quickly as the guy lost patience and rolled over to reach his perch, grabbing a pistol which was hidden under a shelf right by the door.

Alex straightened his arm and took careful aim. A single shot rang out causing everybody to jump six feet in the air. By the time they landed back on earth, a ripple of red cascaded from the guard's knee. Alex wasn't stupid enough to kill the fella even though that was his gut instinct. They were here to rob gold and not assassinate bank personnel. Pete popped his head out from behind the staff-only entrance. A nod to Alex and that was his signal to leave.

"Count to one hundred. If anyone moves before you get to the end or tries to follow us then we'll shoot you dead."

More whimpering, but nobody was fool enough to do anything other than carry on kissing marble. Out the rear, Alex caught up with the brothers and exited out of the back entrance. The wheels were there right in front of him but something was missing.

"Where's the gold?"

"Let's get out of here first and we'll deal with the bullion later."

Alex had little choice but to follow the brothers' lead. That the gold had vanished was not a good sign and all his senses were on high alert. The escape from the bank went smoothly and twenty minutes later, they stopped in a car lot in the middle of nowhere. The fellas poured out of the vehicle and the wheels sped off leaving Alex and the Bunyans stranded on their own.

He scanned around and saw nothing but three black cars, all seemingly empty. If this was an ambush—and it felt like that to Alex —then it was most peculiar because the boys already had the loot. Two long seconds and no one moved a muscle.

"What are we doing here?"

"Alex, we're waiting for a truck. Everything is good."

He eyeballed Pete and Frank, who returned his gaze with an icy expression. He ambled over to one car and leaned against a passenger door, partly to check the vehicle wasn't hiding any machine-gun shaped surprises and partly to move away from the center of the lot. If trouble came calling, Alex didn't want to be surrounded.

Hands in pants pockets, he whistled and waited, watching both brothers for any move they might make. Five minutes passed and nobody had appeared.

"You sure we're in the right place?"

"Funny, Alex. Real funny."

Ten more minutes and still bupkis. Alex couldn't tell if the men were sweating because of the weather or nerves. The mysterious truck was taking its time. Frank whispered something into Pete's ear who nodded in reply. They both glanced at Alex and continued their conversation. He wondered if he should place a hand on his gun but bent down to tie up a shoelace instead. This gave him the opportunity to palm a piece before standing up again. Now he was ready for whatever came his way.

Almost at the same moment that thought flashed though his head, a vehicle approached in the distance. First, they saw the dust on the road and then they heard the rumble of its engine. The truck finally drove into the lot and stopped in between the brothers and Alex so they vanished from view.

He dropped to the ground to stare at visible feet beneath the chassis. A third pair appeared and Pete called out for Alex to come round. Gun poised, he walked over. If they were going to attack, now was the time.

29

PARANOIA IS A wonderful thing and Alex's fears mounted in his head, justified by events, but they were misplaced. The boys had just not told him of a last-minute change of plan and he supervised the removal of the gold from Florida with no further incident.

This meant he, Sarah and the kids could enjoy the first night of Seder, the Passover meal. The Rothsteins invited them over and they could hardly refuse such an offer even though neither of them were exactly religious. That said, Alex did feel a nostalgic twinge for his early childhood amid the memory of the stress of reading out a prayer in front of his entire extended family.

When the Cohens arrived, maids hustled the children into a playroom while Alex and Sarah were taken through to a dining room and Carolyn Greene, Arnold's wife made all the introductions. There was Benny Siegel with a floozy by his side, along with Mr. and Mrs. Lansky, Waxey Gordon plus one, and even Charlie Lucky.

"He's the stranger I couldn't leave at the door," explained Rothstein to the assembled throng, referring to one of the many Passover traditions. Sarah smiled as if getting the joke and Alex nodded like the comment meant something to him.

After cocktails were served and consumed, the children were brought in and everybody sat down at the dining table. There were the two Cohen boys and three Lansky kids but no Rothstein kin.

Waxey's adult daughter put in an appearance just before they settled into their seats.

Arnold led the prayers and made sure the children received enough time to hide a piece of Matzah from the adults as generations of youngsters had done before. The mix of food and religion carried on for the next three hours until the group had eaten their way through the story of Exodus.

Alex found almost all the Hebrew difficult to follow, although Sarah seemed to fare better. The only element he recognized was the *Ma Nishtana*, the prayer from the youngest child past Bar Mitzvah age.

Arnold's fluency reminded Alex of his business partner's Orthodox origins, not that he showed any religious fervor on an ordinary day. Why was this night different from all other nights? Because Arnold was spouting Hebrew.

Once the meal eventually wound down, the women sidled off to talk among themselves and to leave the men alone.

"Freedom is a wonderful thing. We are lucky to live here and now."

Everyone nodded at Arnold's words and stared into their drinks, slowed by the volume of food consumed that night. Alex compared the life he would have experienced if his family had remained back home. Chances were, he, his parents and his siblings would have been killed by now.

The men did their best not to break the magic of the evening and avoided talking business. The trouble was that their work was the glue that kept them together. Alex found it hard to imagine sharing a meal with any of these guys if they didn't have a common interest in bootlegging, prostitution, gambling and drug running. These were happy days for them all.

30

ALEX SPENT MUCH of his time when not in the office back in the Richardson, almost as if he hankered for the simpler life of his early days in the country. In another compartment of his mind, he knew that spending time with his men in a speakeasy meant he was choosing not to spend it with Sarah and his boys.

Once the joint had been refurbished after the Maranzano attack, business returned quickly—its reputation was strong and locals knew it was backed by Alex and his associates. Word soon spread about what happened to the fellas who'd brought mayhem to the place.

Each night the venue buzzed with the sound of coffee cups clinking, filled to the brim with high quality hooch. The Richardson band played the latest tunes for dancing couples and the gaming room at the back occupied those who wanted to play cards while they drank themselves into oblivion. Meanwhile, the second floor unleashed opportunities for the man seeking company and a brew. Every male taste was catered for somewhere in the building.

Alex and his guys hid themselves away from the main room, separated by a two-way mirror so they could keep an eye on customers in case of trouble. Police raids were rare and almost always prearranged but drunks have a habit of escalating disputes into anger too quickly and can scare other johns away.

Ezra had the smarts to realize that the band needed improving. Why would couples go to a show on Broadway if they could come straight to the Richardson? So he paid singers from the most popular shows to do a stint at the club. When word spread, customers arrived two hours earlier and takings soared through the roof. After a few months, Ezra found he could pay the second-rank performers to sing instead and still the tables were full from eight in the evening.

ALEX SPRAWLED ON his favorite chair overlooking the Richardson's drinking room. His crew were still out making collections, having arranged to meet him later. He considered popping home for a short while, but knew the minute he announced his departure, an argument would follow and he didn't have the energy to have another row with Sarah.

The band tooted through some jazz numbers and then a singer took the stage and the mood changed. As soon as she appeared in front of the musicians, the audience applauded and that's what grabbed Alex's attention. As he peered into the darkened auditorium, he saw the sparkling white sequins of a shimmery dress until his eyes followed the contours of her body upwards as he reached her shoulders and head.

He squinted and looked again, then he scowled for a second. Alex didn't waste his time following show business, but he thought he might recognize the singer. His memory flicked through the female faces he'd seen over the years and stopped at one person he'd only observed twice in his life.

Ida Grynberg was a star of the Yiddish theater and had been onstage when he and Sarah had hit a show when he was recovering after the war. He'd also met her before France when he'd fed her opium habit. Both these events felt like ancient history now.

He flipped a switch on the wall and the sounds of the performance rattled through a small speaker near the ceiling. Alex had no ear for music, but he thought she sounded good and the response from the audience showed he was right. Two songs later and he moved to the back of the auditorium at a table of his own.

Now he was able to hear the lilt in her voice properly and could see her curves more easily. Both made him smile, and he noticed a warmth in the pit of his stomach. Alex doubted if Ida knew he was even there so he called a cigarette girl over and asked her to pass a hastily written note to the performer.

Twenty minutes later and she left the stage. A quick change into something more comfortable and Ida appeared at Alex's table, gliding in from nowhere.

"Thanks for the invitation, but have we met before?"

"Yes, but a long time ago under different circumstances. Forgive me, but I have always been an admirer of your work and would be so pleased if you'd do me the honor of sharing a drink with me."

"How could I refuse you, Mr. Cohen?"

"Call me Alex and, please, sit down."

THREE DAYS LATER and Alex let himself into Ida's hotel room. She lay on the bed, fully clothed, with a pipe resting on the carpeted floor. He smiled, sat down on a chair to remove his shoes and messed about with the pipe until a plume of smoke escaped his lungs. Alex slumped next to Ida and allowed the intense joy of the opium to consume him.

After an hour unconscious, he opened one eye and saw only Ida's back. He raised a hand and touched her side but had no energy to do anything else. She was still asleep anyway. He closed his eyelid and returned to the inky blackness of his mind.

When he woke up again, Ida had vanished. Alex sat up with a start but relaxed when he saw her standing at the other side of the bedroom in only her underwear. A smile ripped across his face.

"I'm hungry."

"For me or the steak on my fork?"

"Both. Come here."

She did as she was told and brought the room service plate over. Ida fed him while he toyed with the straps on her camisole. He hadn't been so relaxed with a woman in a bedroom since he first slept with Sarah. And that was years ago.

Alex enjoyed spending time with Ida—she possessed that freewheeling indifference to public opinion, common to those who tread the boards. Her single-minded focus on her career kept her distant from long-term relationships, but that didn't mean she shunned the company of men. Far from it, but she used a pipe to take away the loneliness she felt at the end of every performance.

They remained next to each other until Ida stepped back, removed her clothing and slipped into bed. Alex did the same and thoughts of Sarah fizzled out of his mind.

◆ ◆ ◆

ALEX PUT ON his clothes and glanced at the naked, sleeping Ida. She kept him alive with her wild carefree approach to life. She cared about her audience when onstage but the moment she walked down the steps, she focused entirely on what was important to her: hedonistic, raw experience. Back home, the contrast couldn't have been more stark as soon as he stepped into their hallway.

"I won't ask you where you've been because I am sick and tired of hearing your lies. Just tell me that you spoke with the consultant about David's knee."

The kid had tripped on his own feet the previous week and fallen on the sidewalk. Since then he'd been complaining about a pain in his right leg.

"Not yet but I'll get it sorted. It's been crazy busy at work."

Sarah faltered, pattered up to him and delivered a peck on his cheek. Then she recoiled with anger in her slits for eyes.

"Next time you sleep with someone behind my back at least have the decency to wipe her lipstick off your collar and not stink of her when you enter your family's home."

Alex let Sarah's fists pummel his chest until her energy abated and then he grabbed both her hands and pulled them down by her sides out of the way. This meant they stood inches apart, lips almost touching, staring into each other's eyes.

"I wouldn't be home so late if you showed some interest in me beyond complaining. And the streets are dangerous enough without you trying to hurt me. You need to treat me better before I want to spend more time with you and the boys."

Sarah fled upstairs and Alex heard her sobbing. He popped his head into the playroom and smiled as he watched the boys messing about with the nanny. He didn't interrupt them because they seemed so happy.

Alex hustled over to his bedroom, grabbed a change of clothing and rushed back out. All the while, Sarah's crying echoed around the house.

Over the next four years, Alex and Sarah were intimate four times. Once, the following day, when Alex returned to let Sarah know he had organized a doctor's appointment for David and three other occasions, each of which created another male heir–Asher, Elijah and Arik.

NOVEMBER 1927

31

WHEN THE HOLLAND Tunnel opened on November 12, cars lined up for nearly a mile to pay fifty cents to travel between New York and New Jersey. As vehicles trundled through the darkness of the world's longest road tunnel, Uncle Sam's Treasury was gouging its way through the money made by the Chicago outfit.

The US government's response to the bootlegging industry had been slow, in part because gangs operated beyond state lines and the cops did not. But that didn't mean there was no reaction—the Bureau of Prohibition had been formed and had hired bright men to bring down the hoods who were well organized and making money out of their illegal liquor enterprises.

Much focus was aimed at Chicago because of its relative proximity to the Windsor-Detroit supply line. This hit Alex and his friends square in their wallets, but they also understood that what happened first in the Windy City would be repeated closer to home in Manhattan.

Distilleries were smashed by federal agents and bootleg liquor poured down the drains. None of this was good for business. When the ordinary Joe popped over to a blind pig, they realized they were doing wrong, but surely did not consider themselves engaged in a criminal conspiracy with a bunch of cut-throat gangsters. The newspapers said otherwise. Takings were down and the fellas headed over to Arnold's suite for a meeting.

175

"We must do something about these bureau pinheads."

"What do you suggest, Meyer?"

"Pay them to look the other way. We've done that with the local cops all over the country. These guys out of uniforms need to feed their families, don't they?"

"Alfonse tried what you suggest and still they interrupt his work regularly. There's no reason we'll be more successful."

"Some of us, Alex, have a lower profile than Alfonse. No offense intended, Arnold."

"None taken, Charlie. Reporters seek me out and I respond politely to their questions in the hope they'll go away. Alfonse loves the publicity and the attention he gets from it."

"So what can we do about it?"

"Alex, perhaps the trick is to let them catch us."

"Are you out of your mind, Meyer?"

"Steady, Alex. What I mean is that if we allow the cops to find the odd warehouse or still, then they get the opportunity to call in the press hounds and show them how they are beating us to within an inch of our lives..."

"Meanwhile, we carry on in other locations and everyone is happy."

"While the main heat is in Chicago, we can probably get away with that here. But we need a different solution to protect our Detroit interests."

The men fell silent because Arnold was correct. They could hoodwink some dumb flatfoot with a half-empty warehouse but if the bureau sent any significant manpower over, they'd have a real job to keep all the speakeasies supplied with booze.

Alex decided to find a different place on the Canadian border to ship the booze over. He'd work with Abe Bernstein as they had a common interest in keeping the greenbacks flowing.

The men ironed out several details of the liquor business, as well as a few other matters and eventually they stood up to leave. Arnold asked Alex to stay a short while longer.

"There's something I'd like your assistance with, but I'd rather the others didn't find out."

"How can I help, Arnold?"

"The only thing I ask of anybody who works with me or for me is complete and utter loyalty. Without it, we are nothing. You and I understand this otherwise we would not be in the fortunate positions we find ourselves in."

"For sure. We live together, we fight together, but we die alone."

"Waxey was right. Trouble is that one of my associates has forgotten this simple truth. I have been informed he intends to share his knowledge of our operations with the cops."

"That's easy. A call to a captain in my pay and I can make the whole problem go away."

"If that was all that was required, I would have picked up the phone myself. This fellow is going to the Feds and I need him to be stopped, no matter what."

"Okay. We need to get to the guy before he makes his move."

"Exactly right. He mustn't sing, but whatever you do needs to be conducted without fuss. None of our mutual friends must hear about this or we will unnerve them and our circle of trust will get shattered. Also, we wouldn't want the Feds to come sniffing around later on."

"So he vanishes without trace or dies by natural causes. There aren't any other options that pop into my head."

"You are the right person for this, Alex. Just be aware he will be taken in for questioning tomorrow morning."

"That's not much time."

"Do whatever you need to stop Shlomo Tzvi squealing. Everything else is secondary to me."

THE BUREAU OF Prohibition had told Tzvi they'd collect him by taxi under police protection. Alex reckoned the speed of all this activity was designed to get a signed statement before the fella changed his mind. He was the first guy Alex had known who was prepared to rat on his people.

The ever-reliable Captain Frye furnished Alex with all the details he needed, so he was able to put together a plan before he went to bed in Ida's arms.

Ezra had borrowed a cab and uniform from their haulage interests and had stationed the vehicle outside the bureau offices at just the time Frye had said the Prohibition investigator would head out to meet Tzvi. Alex followed them in his own saloon.

They convoyed across Manhattan and went through the newly painted Holland Tunnel. Tzvi had been smart enough to lie low away from anyone who might have recognized him. Then they headed back the same way until the car sped past Fifth and Seventh Avenue and the Prohi investigator realized something was up.

Too late for him because Ezra locked the passenger doors and didn't stop until they reached the heart of Brownsville, deep in what the locals called Little Jerusalem, but the rest of the world knew as Brooklyn. Ezra stopped the taxi at the corner of Riverdale and Chester Avenue and the two men bustled Tzvi and the Prohi into a nearby building.

Ezra stuffed a gag into each of their mouths so that no one could hear any screams. This precaution was unnecessary because the joint was as empty as sin and the walls were thick and made of brick—no crummy tenement partitions here.

Alex and Ezra slapped Tzvi and the Prohi around a bit to get their attention and to disorient them slightly. Hands tied behind their backs, they were thrown into separate rooms and left lying on the floor in the semi-permanent half-light. With the doors slammed shut, Alex whispered his intentions to Ezra.

"Let's find out if Shlomo has anything to confess. He's on a one-way ticket to hell—and I don't even believe in hell."

"You're a good Jewish boy, of course you don't. What about the other guy?"

"Let's wait a while before deciding whether to kill him."

Alex entered Tzvi's room and kicked him in the kidneys. Then he picked him up by the armpits and slung him onto a chair, the only piece of furniture in the place.

"Why d'you do it, Shlomo?"

"Don't know what you're talking about. I ain't done nothing."

"If you treat me like a fool, then I'll become angry. You were sharing a cab with a Prohibition investigator who was taking you to his headquarters. Explain to me how you got yourself into this situation."

Three short, sharp breaths and Shlomo Tzvi unburdened himself.

"Money was tight and I had to cut a few corners, otherwise there was no food on my family's table. So we get pulled by a Prohi with a truckful of booze and they said they'd throw the book at me—I couldn't afford the fine. Or we could give them some information. Nothing much at first. The location of a truck we'd be using or the address of a warehouse. Then they wanted more and I didn't know what to do. I'd got in so far that I couldn't see a way of getting back. They told me I'd get a subpoena if I refused to cooperate. And here I am."

Alex allowed the dust to settle on the man's words and nodded his head. He understood the fella's situation only too well. If it wasn't for money, we'd all live immaculate lives. Alex shrugged and put his fingers deep into his pants pocket. His right hand retrieved a gun and he whipped the barrel out until it touched Shlomo's forehead. A single crack rang out as Alex squeezed the trigger once and Tzvi's brains blasted over the wall behind him in an almost perfect circle.

Ezra popped his head round the door to check that all was well. Alex signaled everything was fine and walked into the neighboring room. An acrid smell of urine hit his nose as he stepped inside. The man must have wet himself at the sound of the gunfire.

"Help me shift this guy out of here. The stench is unbearable."

Ezra dragged the Prohi out by his hair and along the corridor. At the far end was another empty office with white-painted brickwork and no furniture. Alex brought in three chairs so they could all get comfortable.

"What's your name, cop?"

"William Forster and I'm a Prohibition investigator."

"I asked for your name, not your life story, Bill."

"My name is William..."

A punch to the sternum from Ezra to shut him up and Bill crumpled in two. Alex stood up and sauntered toward the wheezing sack of humanity. He took a grip of the back of Bill's hair and pulled up his head so the guy could look him squarely in the eye.

"Bill. I want you to listen to me carefully. Can you do that for me?"

"Yes."

"Excellent. I need to find out what you got on our mutual friend next door. I'm guessing you were his handler otherwise he wouldn't have trusted you sufficiently to take the ride to your HQ."

Eyes darted left and right as Bill tried to think straight enough to figure out what to say.

"Yes."

"So what do you know, Bill?"

"Nothing. I mean, he was a reliable source and had come good for us five or six times. We leaned on him a bit and he folded like a cheap suit. We hadn't interviewed him yet. There's not much else I can say."

"Did he tell you who he worked for, for example?"

"No. We asked, but he was too scared. He demanded protection before he'd squawk."

"I believe you, Bill, because Shlomo was a coward and a family man. He wouldn't have wanted to put his wife and children in harm's way. As you heard, his family has lost a father, husband and provider. Do you have kith and kin, Bill?"

"A wife. We were planning on having children next year."

Alex smiled and Bill returned the expression. Then he blasted a hole in Bill's chest; he gurgled briefly and slumped onto the floor.

"Call some reliable guys to get this mess cleared up. I'm going back to the city. I'd forgotten how much I hate Brooklyn."

SMOKE. MUD. BLOOD. One moment his lips were pressed against the soil, the next Alex was scurrying along the ground, hauling himself forward by the elbows. Five feet, then ten. All the time he altered his direction based on where he could locate Bobby's screams.

Another five feet and bullets zinged across the muddy space between Alex and his friend. Eventually the strafing ceased, and he made it to lie by Bobby's side. The guy was blubbering and screaming alternately.

"Bobby, you'll be fine. I'm here now."

Alex said those words before he'd raised his head to assess how Bobby was doing. The man's body was a pool of blood surrounded by limbs. How could something as small as a bullet do so much damage to one person?

More strafing and when the sniper rested, Alex looked up again. The German was only forty feet ahead and Alex had seen enough flashes from the soldier's rifle to know precisely where he was. When he turned to look at Bobby, his friend was silent.

"Bobby?"

Dead. Alex felt a tear drip off his cheek and then he dug in, using Bobby's corpse as a shield. Training his scope on the location from where the sniper had been firing, Alex waited. He saw soil, grass trampled underfoot, mud and then a slight glint which told him the guy was still there, getting ready for another assault.

Only this time, Alex aimed at where that reflection had been and squeezed off a round. Then he stood by. For ten, twenty, thirty seconds but nothing. He raised his head slightly but nobody fired at him. He shuffled his way over and found the German corpse with a bullet in his skull. Seventeen years old, Alex reckoned, and a leg blown off in some earlier skirmish. They gave him a medal for taking so long to murder the cripple that he let Bobby die...

32

ARNOLD THANKED ALEX when he reported back later in the day, having cleaned himself up and dusted himself down. He made a mental note to share Arnold's financial appreciation with Ezra, who had done all the hard work with virtually no notice.

The consequences of their journey to Brownsville lasted much longer than the trip back to the Lower East Side. Bill's disappearance took two days to get noticed. By the time his superiors had filed a missing person report, Shlomo and Bill's bodies were propping up the foundations of a building in the Bronx, a residential block being constructed by one of Arnold's investments.

That meant the cops had to resort to breaking down doors and generally making a nuisance of themselves. Funny thing was that the Prohis were not taking bribes—for the first time since the Volstead Act came into force. The orders came from high up and landed on the heads of the low-paid investigators with a very clear message: get the scum who attacked one of our own. Nobody spoke for Tzvi, whose widow received a pension from Arnold on account of his mysterious vanishing.

Then the retaliation began. Every warehouse the Prohis thought might contain a crate of liquor was raided. Heads were cracked and fresh supplies were met at the bridges or tunnels into the town.

There wasn't a gang on Manhattan that didn't suffer. From Harlem in the north to Wall Street at the tip of the island, business was down and prospects were bleak. The Italians, the Jews and what was left of the Irish and German gangs were finding out what happened when federal investigators joined forces with local flatfeet. Not even Frye would answer Alex's calls.

◆ ◆ ◆

"HOW LONG DO you think we can take this heat?"

"Alex, the cops aren't letting up. I can't see how we'll survive this for very much longer."

"Let's not get alarmist, Meyer. The Feds bend with the wind. All we do is wait for something to happen at the other end of the country and then resources will be flung over there as a knee-jerk reaction to some other calamity befalling this once great nation."

"Easy for you to say, Arnold, as you possess the reserves to lean on beyond anything the rest of us can muster."

"Tell your people to lie low. Keep a skeleton staff at each of your speakeasies and soak up any income from prostitution, gaming and union protection. The Feds understand that if they remove gambling, sex and alcohol from the law-abiding Joe then there'll be riots in the streets. Even the goyim won't stand for that."

"These problems would vanish in an instant if they found the guy who offed the Prohi."

"Let's not talk like that, Charlie. They want to divide us but we will always be stronger than that. We are a union."

"We live together, we fight together and we die alone."

Charlie Lucky sipped his drink and the others fell silent too. Arnold and Alex were the only two who knew what had really happened and how close all the guys in the suite had got to serving hard time if Tzvi had spilled his guts, because the chain of command led straight to the four fellas.

"That may be so, Arnold, but the other gangs are fit to burst. They might not prove anything but word on the street was that Alex executed the hit on your orders. I'm not saying they're right or wrong. Doesn't matter either way, but they are acting like it's true."

"Let them bleat."

"Easy to say, Alex, but Maranzano has put out a hit on you both. Others are holding fire, but you two have unfinished business from a few years back and he's fixing to sort everything."

"Charlie, is that for certain?"

"That's straight from reliable sources. I got dealings with Maranzano so I learn things I probably shouldn't. From what I can tell, it's a matter of days before a rifle is trained on you or you're found hanged with a knife in your back outside City Hall."

Alex cast a glance at Arnold, who threw a worried smile in his direction. The vultures were circling.

ARNOLD ROTHSTEIN LEFT for a vacation in Florida under Charlie's protection. Everyone figured the Big Bankroll would be safer if he laid low for a while and Miami-Dade county seemed the best place for him to rest. There were enough of Charlie's business partners operating casinos there for Arnold to not only remain far away from any trouble but be entertained along the way.

Alex could not say the same. Although nobody said it, he felt they blamed him for their current troubles, even though he was only acting on behalf of the Big Bankroll. Arnold had coached Charlie since he was a boy so it was the Italian who explained how Alex should stay in town and face the heat else the gangs would follow Arnold south and who knew what would happen.

Charlie was right; they needed a worm to catch their fish but Alex wasn't happy about being left to dangle on the line. Maranzano alone had proved himself to be a formidable foe who would stop at nothing to see him dead. Their altercation over the Richardson was small potatoes compared to the revenue loss they were suffering now.

What Alex didn't want to admit to himself was that his ego drove him to remain in Manhattan too. There was no way he was going to allow himself to be sent packing by a bunch of hoods. This was his city and he would live in it until he was good and ready to leave. And not a moment before. This hubris almost made him forget those around him.

"You and Massimo should take a vacation in Windsor or somewhere safe. If they come gunning for me, there's no need for you to get caught in the crossfire."

"We'll be okay, Alex. I've got informants listening in every drinking hole from here to Central Park. As soon as they do anything, we'll know about it."

"And we're bringing in some fresh blood from Chicago and Detroit. These old men have enjoyed the easy life for too long. Typical, they feel a little heat down their necks, they panic. Their days are numbered. The moment has come for a new generation to step forward."

For the first moment in a week, Alex headed home to check on his family. Sarah sat in the living room and the kids played somewhere in the apartment. She glanced up from her book, half-smiled and returned to her story. Alex squatted on a stool next to her and placed a hand on her knee. With that, she looked straight at him and closed her novel.

"What's the matter, Alex?"

"I can't be sure, but things might get ugly."

"How bad?"

"There are business interests aligning against us."

"You don't need to talk to me like I'm one of your people. What's happening?"

Alex stared into her eyes and saw concern reflected back.

"I did some work for Arnold which meant the police have descended on the city. He's off to lie low for a while and I need to take the heat for him."

"You're fighting the cops?"

"Oh, no. It's the other bosses. They are losing money hand over fist and blame me."

"Will they kill you?"

"They'll give it a damn good try but I have too many people looking out for me to let that happen, hon'."

"I don't want to start an argument with you, honestly, but why suddenly come back here to tell me this?"

"Because I don't want you and the boys to get hurt. For your own safety, I think you should move out of the city until this has blown over."

"Where? For how long?"

"I don't want to be too dramatic, but Canada. There's a town called Windsor close to the border. It's only a few hours from here and it's under my control."

"Should we pack for a weekend?"

"Assume weeks rather than days, but it could all blow over in a short while. This is a precaution. Nothing more."

"And I suppose we should leave tonight? I mean, that would unsettle the kids most, wouldn't it?"

"Tomorrow. The day after at the latest. Give them time to get used to the idea, but go. I need to focus all my energies on sorting this out and can't afford to become sidetracked worrying about you."

"I never knew you cared."

33

THREE DAYS AFTER Sarah and the children traveled to Windsor, Maranzano made his first move. His men attacked the Richardson and, when Alex stepped inside, he experienced a terrible flashback but had learned enough in the intervening years not to retaliate but to sit and wait instead. His hours with Arnold were not wasted and the spirit of the street thug, Waxey was receding.

Alex spent the time preparing for the inevitable attack. The next day, he opened up a new venue on the other side of Madison Square, with metal bars over the frontage and a steel door, all hidden behind wooden fencing, until now. Clients entered easily but it could be closed down to outsiders immediately—unwelcome gangs or the cops alike.

Within a day, his old customers had found their way over to the new Richardson. The stage was smaller and Ida was none too happy, but a fur coat changed her countenance and Alex and his fellas carried on business as usual.

Two days later and the beer stopped flowing. No matter what route they used, Alex, Meyer and Charlie couldn't get their trucks into Manhattan. They even looked at using trains but as soon as they sent the first haul down the tracks, Maranzano's men robbed the train leaving blood on the line. Ezra and Massimo hit back with three groups of fellas who headed backstage at a number of Maranzano cathouses and slashed the face of every nafka they saw.

The response was swift and brutal. The old Sicilian sent his guys to ransack warehouses and trucks, shooting at any fella in the vicinity. This was a bloodbath on the New York streets which even the politicians were unable to ignore. Headlines screamed for the authorities to take action and Alex decided it was time to oblige.

"WE MUST CLIP this Mustache Pete. The old timer has gone too far."

Ezra and Massimo nodded in agreement, sick and tired of sitting on their hands the past week.

"Maranzano has been taking liberties at our expense."

"True. The fault lies at our door for the heat that's raining down on our fair city but I have tolerated this for long enough. Today we take the fight to Maranzano."

Alex described his plan until the two men understood what they needed to do and how they would win the war and not just the next battle. With everyone clear, they set to work.

Mulberry Street lay three blocks west of the Bowery and you would be forgiven for thinking you'd moved country if you took a walk along Grand Street. From the warmth of the shtetl to the cold winds of Little Italy in the length of twenty paces. The Hebrew lettering on the signage vanished and was replaced with the language of southern Europe.

Onward they marched until Massimo's gang arrived at Maranzano's headquarters at Mulberry and Broome. Within thirty seconds, Ezra's men appeared from the north and they waited for the signal. Right on cue, Alex appeared in his car, screeched to a halt and let rip with automatic gunfire, each slug tearing a little more away from the frontage.

By the time the vehicle zoomed off and Alex pulled in round the corner, a hail of bullets was erupting out of the building, aimed at nowhere in particular. Everyone kept their heads down and waited again. These fellas knew better than to make a move with so much death flying around the streets.

Eventually the Maranzano guns fell silent but Ezra and Massimo did nothing. Alex sensed the tension in the air he breathed as his men were itching to respond. Instead they waited for an eternity. Each inhalation and exhalation took a lifetime.

With every civilian having fled the neighborhood as soon as the first shot rang out, there was nothing to hear except your own lungs. Then the astute men in the building would have sensed a low rumble, which built in volume over the following five minutes. Before they realized where the noise was coming from, they found themselves surrounded—not just by the twenty guys who walked over with Ezra and Massimo, but by at least sixty more.

From where had these troops come? Chicago and Detroit. Alex knew the difficulties in the Lower East Side were hurting Alfonse and Abe as much as Meyer, Charlie and Arnold. So he'd placed two phone calls and asked for support. And here it was.

Having pinned Maranzano down inside his headquarters, Ezra's men cut the phone line and then the power cable too. Now the head of the snake was isolated, some of the Sugar House gang peeled off to ransack Maranzano property. Alex had previously furnished Abe with a list of venues and Abe picked professionals who could be guaranteed not to lose their heads and go on some kind of rampage. For Alex, this was a military campaign.

Abe's men returned at dusk at which point Alfonse's fellas took their leave of the main scene and assaulted the places on their list. As the sun rose, there were still forty fellas surrounding Mulberry and Broome with the remaining number taking a rest. They were in this for the long haul and Alex had prepared his guys to expect the siege to last for days not hours.

The one group Alex normally would have relied on was the cops, but because they'd created this situation by not turning their usual blind eye, he'd put in place a different plan for them.

While Tammany Hall's influence had reduced over the decades, the powerhouse still held sway and the politicians earned their kickbacks. Arnold helped Alex meet the right guy to have a quiet word. The cops would spend their time attending to the venues which were attacked and somehow Maranzano's corner of paradise would be left alone.

By noon, a voice shouted out that they wanted to have a discussion and one by one, the streets were vacated with only hundreds of empty shells on the ground to remind anyone that there had been any action there at all. That and every wall and pane of glass being shot to hell.

The military campaign turned Little Italy into a war zone for a day but the truce held, not just for the next few nights but even after Alfonse and Abe's men had gone home. Past Chanukah and on toward Passover.

APRIL 1928

34

THE DUST SETTLED on the street battles of the previous year but no one was foolish enough to believe that everything had been forgotten. Arnold returned to the city in time for his traditional New Year party and Alex brought Sarah along, despite her misgivings. And who could blame her?

As soon as the Passover festivities were over, Charlie updated Alex on the latest news from the Maranzano crew.

"Word on the street is that Maranzano wants you dead."

"There's bad blood there, for sure. I thought Maranzano might have let things go as we are all making money again and it was only ever business."

"Don't take this the wrong way but you do not understand because you are Jewish. The Sicilian in this Mustache Pete will never forget and never forgive. It's not in his nature."

"It's a vendetta; I get it."

"Like you have no idea. The trouble is that I can't help protect you. My position is supported by Maranzano even though Arnold and I do a lot of business together. You must find another way to take care of this problem."

"If you find out more, will you at least let me know?"

"Naturally. I just need to be careful that Maranzano doesn't get wise."

Alex needed to get some muscle behind him—and something that had more influence than a bunch of fellas with machine guns. He'd done that before but the old Sicilian was like a wasp in his ear.

Half a century before Alex arrived in the land of the free, the Democratic Party had wrestled control of New York though a simple cocktail of intimidation and bribery; both delivered by the gangs that ran the street corners. The center of the Democrats in Manhattan was Tammany Hall, so that was the natural place for Alex to head. If he could get the politicians behind him, then Alex could use their sway to keep Maranzano off his back.

George W. Olvany had become boss of Tammany Hall four years earlier and had instituted a series of grifts to line his pockets and those of his friends and business associates. Arnold mixed in his circles so, by extension, Alex secured a meeting with the man who decided who would be Mayor of New York.

"I understand your problem, Alex, and there is nothing I would like more than to help one of Arnold's friends."

"That is great news. No one in Tammany looked good during the November troubles. Who wanted to celebrate Thanksgiving with so much blood on the street...?"

"...and liquor flowing down the drains."

"Exactly right. What a waste all round, but my sources tell me that certain individuals are planning to settle old scores and I hope you agree that this fine city has no need for that bloodletting."

"This is not Chicago."

"So can you help me clip Maranzano's wings?"

The former judge sipped his tea laced with gin and considered his options.

"The question isn't whether I am able to give you the assistance you crave; of course I can. Tammany Hall and your kind have been doing business for years. You and I need to reach some accommodation to grease the machinery to resolve this matter in your favor."

Alex sighed as quietly as he could muster. With these men and their municipal and government job titles, it always boiled down to how much gelt they would get today. They could never see beyond the end of their noses. Their beaks were buried so deep in the trough, they could barely breathe.

"Do you have a figure in mind, George?"

"Well, a one-off donation would be appreciated and enable me to mobilize appropriate forces at my disposal."

"The payments we make every month aren't enough?"

"Alex, you sound as though you begrudge our arrangement."

"Not at all. I'm finding it hard to understand what I get for my money."

"Peace of mind. You sleep soundly in your mistress's bed at night knowing the cops won't burst through the door and take you away with your shorts around your ankles."

Olvany scribbled on a piece of paper, folded it and pushed it over to Alex, who opened it and stared at the handwritten number. It was ridiculously high. Greed oozed out of every digit. Alex allowed himself a snort of laughter. He didn't like this Tammany boss and his Waspish manner.

"I appear to have wasted both of our time, George. I asked you for aid and you've offered me a trade at a price I am not prepared to pay."

"ALEX, ONE OF my men tells me Maranzano has brought in a Jew to his crew; that's never happened before."

"Any idea about this guy, Charlie?"

"None. I haven't seen him and Maranzano never mentioned the fella, but my informant has never been wrong."

"Should I be worried?"

"The Mustache Pete has never had any time for Jews. The Sicilian only trusts people from the island."

"Until now, it would seem. Looks like I will have to take the fight to Maranzano once and for all."

BACK IN HIS office, squirreled away inside the depths of an anonymous building, Alex took stock of the situation with Massimo and Ezra.

"If we do nothing, then one day soon they'll discover me with a bullet in my head."

"We've got you covered. There's an extra security detail in place and we have eyes on every street corner."

"Ezra, that's good to know but I can't live my life like this. We need to know the threat is over."

"How do you want us to do that?"

"Massimo, I wish I had an answer but I don't know. Short of driving over and shooting the guy, my mind's a blank."

"You want me to do it?"

"No! Such a direct assault on the man won't solve anything. There'll always be another Maranzano. What we need to do is figure out how to remove his sort from the world. One bullet is no solution."

They were silent for a spell as each of the three did their best to square the circle. At one level, Alex wanted to get Chicago and Detroit behind him again and annihilate the Maranzano clan but he understood how Abe did business with them, as did Arnold. So that would never be acceptable to his many partners. There had to be a way though; he couldn't take the thought of sitting in that room waiting to die.

"Why don't we call for a meeting to clear the air, then whack everyone who shows up?"

"And, Massimo, what's stopping anybody who survives that slaughter visiting us the following day? If you're going to make a suggestion at least think it through first."

"Sorry, boss."

Then Alex's phone rang, and Arnold's voice requested the pleasure of his company in his suite at his earliest convenience.

"One of you guys come with me. I've got to visit a friend."

◆ ◆ ◆

ARNOLD, MEYER AND Charlie were sitting down, slowly sinking into the leather seating when Alex walked in. Benny Siegel paced behind the couch housing Arnold and Charlie. The man never stopped walking the whole time. His continual movement added a sense of urgency which would otherwise have been missing from the room, given their discussions.

"Thanks for popping over, Alex. We've got some matters we need to discuss."

Alex chose a comfortable chair and lounged in it, conscious that all eyes were aimed at him and knowing this casual request had to have something to do with Maranzano. Charlie found it particularly hard to maintain eye contact with him; a sure sign of trouble ahead.

"What's on your mind, Arnold?"

"Just some business we need to put in order."

Benny barged into the center of the group forcing Alex and Arnold to break eye contact.

"Can we please get to the point? Alex, you must stop gunning for Maranzano as it's bad for all our businesses."

"How about stopping Maranzano? From what I understand, the Mustache Pete has put a hit out on me. Arnold, you've invited the wrong fella over. You should tell Maranzano he should stand down."

"That won't happen, Alex. Maranzano is a made man and is untouchable."

"Charlie, I know. And that's why Benny wants to cut to the chase. He can smell the Italian outfit breathing down his neck."

"Don't be like that, Alex, and Benny stop wearing a hole in my rug and sit down."

Siegel walked over and slumped in a spare chair. Throughout this time, he spun his hat round the fingers of one hand. Meanwhile, Arnold did his best to keep the atmosphere calm even though Alex looked daggers at anyone who spoke.

"We understand you've been talking to Tammany Hall, and that isn't good for business. Politicians are only interested in grifting and not in anything else."

"I was checking out what options I have. You are right, Arnold. All that happened was that Olvany tried a shakedown, so I walked away."

Then the phone rang, and all heads turned to the sound of its bell. Arnold sauntered over and picked up the device from the receiver. Within a minute, he'd replaced the handset and walked over to Alex. Then he tapped him on his jacket shoulder.

"You need to get home. Looks like someone has taken your youngest."

35

"THEY TOOK ARIK an hour ago."

"Tell me exactly what happened, hon'."

"I was shopping and the kids were out with Leah."

"Who?"

"Leah Rinat, our maid."

"Is that normal?"

"Yes, Alex. The three youngest go out with her most afternoons, weather permitting. Anyway, they were in the park and some guy rushed up, grabbed Arik and ran off."

With those words, Sarah began to sob again and Alex held her in his arms until the tears subsided.

"Do you trust Leah?"

"Of course. What a question."

"Have a think before you answer me, Sarah. Can we trust Leah?"

She remained silent for several seconds before responding.

"I thought I did, but now you're asking me with that voice, I'm not certain. She brought references and has been nothing but helpful. Maybe she's just been biding her time."

"Don't worry either way. I'll get Ezra to have a quiet word with her and we'll check out her story."

"What are you planning to do?"

"Just talk and nothing else. You need not be concerned. She won't be harmed no matter what. Chances are she's clean."

"Promise?"

"I do. The most important issue right now is to find out where Arik is and to bring him home."

"Do you know who has done this terrible thing? He's only two years old."

"Not yet. We will and I shall get him back."

Alex met Ezra in the kitchen for a private word. While he had no clue who might have physically kidnapped his son, you didn't need to be a genius to see the person pulling the strings was Salvatore Maranzano. From the way Arnold touched him on the shoulder, Alex knew that his trusted friend had figured it out too before he'd even put the phone down.

"Make some enquiries, Ezra. Find out if our maid was involved. Be very gentle with her because she may be completely innocent."

"And if she's not?"

"Extract all the information you can from her and ensure she meets with an accident. Sarah must suspect nothing, so let the calamity happen next month."

"Understood, boss. You reckon this has anything to do with business?"

"Of course. Any normal kidnapping and we would have received a call by now demanding a ransom to be paid. The fact the phone hasn't rung screams out who is the culprit."

"Maranzano."

"Yep, but that doesn't tell us where they are holding Arik. I have to know and fast."

"I'll ask Charlie Lucky if he's heard anything today."

"Okay. Get Massimo to send out his men. Scour Central Park for witnesses and I will see if Frye can earn his fee this week."

An hour later, Alex had calmed down Sarah enough so that he felt he could leave her alone. He left one of his foot soldiers at the apartment and hightailed out of the joint. For all that time, no call came through, which confirmed Alex's belief that Maranzano was behind this.

He returned to his office and did his best to wait. Alex knew his men would do their jobs and get him an address, but he wanted it to happen now, so he could regain the sense of control that Maranzano had snatched away from him along with his child.

Ezra passed him a coffee but all he could do was to stare at the drink until it got cold. Alex ground his molars and did his best to get Arik's image out of his mind. Then Massimo popped his head round the door and whispered in Ezra's ear, all the while his eyes peered at Alex. More whispers back and Ezra uncrossed his legs.

"We have news."

"Spill."

"Two of our guys spotted three Maranzano fellas with a kid matching Arik's description."

"Where?"

"Washington and Vestry."

"West side. Near Pier 29?"

"That's the one. A warehouse like any other on the street."

"And not in Maranzano's territory. That means he's getting protection."

"Let's not worry about those details right now and focus on bringing him out safely."

"I know; just expressing a thought. Time to go fishing near the Hudson."

TWENTY MINUTES LATER, Alex, Ezra and Noga Menahem stood on the opposite side of the street from an unassuming entrance with a sign above the door announcing 'Reilly Parts Inc'.

"Any idea how many more beyond the three you saw go in with my boy?"

"No one has come in or out since I arrived here. It looks like a disused husk of a building. Used to be a printing press back in the day."

"In that case, let's pay them a visit."

Alex sent Noga round the rear while he and Ezra searched for a way to get in without knocking on the front door. On the side, facing the river, was an open window on the first floor. Ezra pushed his arm through the gap and unlocked the adjacent pane of glass. A kick through the adjoining strut created a big enough space for both men to get through.

They crouched in the room, an office with desks, chairs and all the usual crap of a normal business that had gone bust. A thick layer of dust formed a patina of dirt across everything they touched. Alex listened at the door but heard nothing on the other side so gingerly he turned the creaking doorknob and popped his head into the corridor. No sign of anyone or anything.

Ezra and Alex crept along the empty passageway, checking on every room they went past. Out into a main reception area which led onto more offices on the other side. Still nothing. A set of stairs headed up to the second floor and another down to the basement. Ezra gestured up or down to Alex, who responded by pointing to the second floor. A nod and they scampered upstairs.

The stairwell opened up into a vast space filled with derelict printing machines. Some had paper inside them as though they had been abandoned halfway through publishing the local newspaper. Others were plain empty.

From nowhere, Alex's ears pricked to attention as he heard Arik's muffled voice. It sounded frightened and Ezra grabbed his shoulder to offer him support—and to prevent him from dashing off and doing something foolish in the heat of the moment.

Ezra's eyes flitted to the far side of the plant and Alex nodded. Still silent, they scurried over until they caught sight of a more open area near a window. With his hands bound by string and a gag stuffed in his mouth, Arik sat whimpering. Three men stood nearby, towering over the little boy. Alex felt the muscles in his arms tense and he gripped his gun even tighter.

ALEX COULD SEE the three guys were carrying pieces and there was no way he could guarantee Arik would survive if he started shooting. At this point, Noga arrived on the scene to even up the numbers. Despite his appearance, there was still too much danger in firing at will. They needed to get closer.

Noga edged ahead using a printing press as cover. Alex followed on behind, realizing he had a good idea. By the time Noga stopped shuffling forward, Alex had a clear line of sight on two of the three kidnappers, but that was not enough. One bullet was all that it would take to kill his little boy.

Meantime, Ezra had positioned himself the other side of the printing press and Alex espied the top of his head bobbing just above the machinery. Arik kicked off, whimpering more, and Alex snapped.

He squeezed the trigger and a slug spat out of the barrel and landed squarely in the chest of the nearest guy. Before he had the chance to crumple onto the ground his companion straightened his shooting arm and inhaled before firing his piece, and that was his mistake. Noga sent a bullet to his heart and a third shot rang out.

For a second, Alex couldn't tell quite what had happened. He blinked and saw his son sitting still in his chair but he had no idea if he was alive or dead. A blur of movement and the third guy ran past and away. Ezra and Noga gave chase leaving Alex to leap forward and wrestle Arik free from the handkerchief stuffed into his mouth and to undo the ropes tying his wrists and feet.

Alex picked his boy up in his arms and ran him down the steps and out onto the sidewalk. Into his car and back home so Arik could bask in the warmth of his mother's embrace. Before anyone could say a word, Alex smiled at the scene before him, turned and walked out to return to Pier 29.

Ezra stood on the street corner but Alex couldn't see Noga anywhere.

"What's cooking?"

"We chased the guy into a building half a block from here. Noga's keeping watch."

"How can one man cover all the entrances?"

"You'll see. It's fine, we've cornered him."

They hustled along the street while they spoke until they reached a low wall, behind which was a single-story construction. A door, a window and not much else to make it stand out, it looked as though it used to be an office but like the Reilly printers, the joint had seen better days.

"Noga said there's no back entrance. He hung round this neighborhood when he was a kid. He robbed from these places so he knows what he's talking about. Our guy has fled into a dead end."

Alex grinned and pulled out his gun. Ezra followed him until they caught up with Noga.

"You wait here a short while; it's time for me to have a conversation with this man."

The two men readied themselves in case of trouble, but kept their hands in their pockets because they couldn't imagine Alex needing any help.

He stormed toward the door, checking left and right for any sign of his quarry. A kick and the wood ripped off its hinges, then he trained his gun into the gloomy darkness ahead of him. A crash and Alex ran down the hallway and arrived at a far room whose door was wide open. Pointing his pistol into the space in front of him, he edged inside and stopped at the sight of a man standing by a desk, staring back at him like a rabbit caught in the lights of an oncoming truck.

Alex aimed his gun low and fired at one ankle causing blood to splat outwards just as the guy fell down and squealed with the pain of the bullet tearing through his flesh. Alex rushed forward and slammed his foot on the guy's wrist, forcing him to let go of his own firearm.

Then Alex dragged him by the scruff of his neck out of the room, down the corridor and out onto the street. Ezra and Noga grabbed him by the arms and led him away with Alex in tow. They bundled him into the back of the car and bombed across town until they reached the other side of the city and a quiet empty warehouse on home turf.

"WHY?"

Brunello Masi stared at Alex but remained silent.

"Why did you steal my son?"

Nothing. Cold eyes bored into Alex's skull.

"Who told you to do it? There's no way it was your idea."

Still no response, which made Alex well up with anger. He lunged forward, fingers forming a fist, and slammed a punch into Masi's face, so forceful that two teeth flew out and landed on the floor, causing a trickle of blood to drip out of the corner of his mouth.

"You'd better understand one thing. You tried to harm my boy and the only reason you are alive is because I know it was not your idea. So what you need to do is spill your guts before I cut you a new hole."

"I'm not giving up nobody."

Alex pulled out a blade and stabbed the knife deep into Masi's thigh; he released a bloodcurdling yelp that subsided into a whimper. Alex kneeled down so his mouth was next to Masi's left ear and whispered, "Who?"

The guy clenched his teeth and tried to purse his lips as best he could. No name was forthcoming so Alex stood up and smiled.

"Watch him."

Then he walked out of the building and returned thirty minutes later with a bag. Masi looked quizzically at him, beads of sweat falling from his forehead. His eyes opened wide when Alex swiveled round to reveal a screwdriver in his hand.

"The choice is yours. Tell me what I want to know or take the consequences."

The man's irises reflected his inner conflict. If he didn't give up a name, he faced a long period of pain and almost certain death from his inevitable injuries or Alex's anger. If Masi ratted his boss out, then he had a chance of living today, but the only way he could survive until morning was to skip town and never return. Even then, he'd spend the rest of his life not knowing if his next breath would be his last.

"If I tell you, will you let me live?"

"Speak the truth and I'll not only spare your soul but I shall give you some scratch and a train ticket to New Jersey. That way you'll be able to get out of town and vanish."

His eyes flitted side-to-side again as Masi weighed up his odds. He swallowed hard and tried to clear his throat but choked instead. Alex indicated to Ezra who took out a bottle and poured a few drops onto Masi's awaiting tongue. A smile briefly appeared on his face and vanished almost immediately as he remembered where he was and why he was there.

"Shmuel Hayyim."

"Who the hell…?"

"Shmuel Hayyim. He's in with Maranzano."

"Never heard of him and since when did that cockroach work with Jews?"

Without waiting for an answer, Alex dug the screwdriver into Masi's stomach and then yanked it out with a twist.

"Make me believe you."

"It's the truth. Maranzano has let a Yid into his outfit. None of us know why but there it is. If I give up an Italian, you'll find out and I'm a dead man for sure. You gotta believe me."

Alex eyeballed Masi and then turned to face Ezra, one eyebrow raised. His friend nodded and glanced at Masi who winced. There was a river of blood pouring out of the guy's body.

"I believe you. We'll take you to a medic we know and then get you out of the city."

"Thank you."

Those were the last words Brunello Masi uttered because Alex took his gun out of his pants pocket, shoved it next to Masi's temple and squeezed the trigger.

"Clear this mess up. I'm going back to be with my family."

36

ALEX WAS NO sooner through the door than Sarah stormed towards him, anger in her eyes and her body language. Before she opened her mouth, Alex could see how she felt.

"What the hell is going on, Alex?"

"How's Arik doing?"

"Just fine under the circumstances; no thanks to you."

"I got him home safe and sound."

"Don't talk to me like I'm some kind of moron. Yes, you brought him back but the only reason he was taken in the first place was because of you... and your business."

Sarah spat out the last two words with utter disdain. She stood at the other side of the hallway, almost as though she couldn't bring herself to be physically near him. Alex attempted to maintain his authority but she had a point, even though he had no intention of admitting that to her.

"The money I make means we can afford a place like this. Don't sneer at our success."

He stared Sarah down and clenched his jaw.

"Has he said anything about what happened?"

"Nothing. Hasn't spoken since he came home."

"Eaten?"

"A slice of *matzah*, but nothing else. He's hidden himself in his bedroom."

Alex nodded and sighed. He knew this conflict would get them nowhere. Instead, he walked toward Arik's room and Sarah followed without trying to stop him. Her fight wasn't with him at all, just frustration at not being able to keep the children safe.

Arik sat on the floor, playing with a fire truck. When his parents entered, he looked up for a second but carried on rocking the toy back and forth. Alex plonked himself next to his son and Sarah went the other side.

"Scary day, huh?"

Arik nodded and continued to move the toy round the floor.

"You were very brave. The way you handled yourself with those men."

Alex casually put an arm around his son and dangled his hand on the boy's shoulder. He leaned into his father with both hands still gripping his toy. Sarah reached out and planted a palm on his leg to show she cared too.

"Can you remember them saying anything to you while you were with them?"

Arik shrugged in silence. A minute later, he asked: "Did you kill them?"

"You don't have to worry your pretty little head about anything like that."

"Will they be back?"

"No, you'll never see them again, you can be certain of that."

Sarah's body stiffened as the conversation turned to what had happened in the warehouse. Arik had said nothing and Ezra had skated round the truth, clearly not sure how much he should impart.

"I saw blood come out of the men."

"We had to get you away from those no-goods because they wouldn't let you go."

"Is that why your friends and you had guns?"

"The most important thing was to make certain you were safe. What happened to them didn't matter."

"Are they dead?"

"That's why you don't have to worry about them coming back."

"Did you kill them?"

"Are you hungry? Your mama said you haven't eaten much since you got home."

"Shall we get you some lokshun soup?"

Arik's face lit up at the mention of his favorite food and Sarah took him by the hand to the dining room while the housekeeper heated some up from her earlier mealtime efforts. Alex followed the two out of the bedroom and made a quick phone call before he joined them for some lokshun. It reminded him of being a kid back in the old country. Now he had his own children to feed.

Once Arik had consumed as much as his stomach would allow, Sarah took him to bed. The boy was exhausted and didn't know it, so there were tears before he eventually settled down to sleep. Alex moved into the sitting room and lounged on a couch, the fingertips of one hand spread out resting on his forehead.

"You tired?"

"Yeah, rescuing children takes it out of you."

"Did you find out who organized the attack?"

"Yep. They'll get theirs, don't you worry, hon'."

"Before you kill them, make them hurt."

"I didn't think you liked the way I resorted to violence."

"I don't but Arik just told me how frightened he was until he saw his daddy standing in the gloom. Why did they take our Arik?"

"A foolish man attacked my family when he should have just gone for me. He will pay for that mistake."

"Make him scream for mercy. Let the momzer learn about pain and anguish."

"Stop talking like that. You've never once acted as though violence was the answer to any of our problems and you shouldn't do it this time. It's turning you... ugly."

Alex didn't have the right words to describe how she made him feel but it was unsettling. She abhorred his aggression and the way he'd achieved his success. For her to speak like that unnerved him. He had to get away, so he stood up and walked out of the apartment, leaving her dazed and confused on the couch.

AND INTO IDA'S arms. Alex's first thought was to check into a hotel but then he realized he wanted to be apart from Sarah but not alone and he was not prepared to spend money on a nafka. She might not have been expecting him—he didn't call ahead—but Ida hid her annoyance reasonably well.

She had readied herself for bed before Alex's arrival and clung to a dressing gown wrapped tightly around her body. Alex walked past her and headed straight for the drinks cabinet. He poured himself a vodka tonic and offered Ida a Cosmo, although he didn't have the energy to mix the cocktail.

Luckily, Ida declined his offer and accepted a vodka tonic instead. They settled down on the couch in her suite and she let him talk himself out of his anger about the day. She sat there and smiled. Eventually, she relaxed her shoulders and uncrossed her arms. Once Alex had wound himself down, Ida offered a few soothing words and pointed out that she had to get up early. He shrugged in complete disinterest but took the hint when she got up and padded over to the bedroom door.

"You coming or have you only turned up at my doorstep to complain about your wife?"

FEBRUARY 1929

37

MEYER, CHARLIE, BENNY and Alex sat in a back booth at Lindy's to commemorate the seven-month anniversary of the death of their close friend and business partner, Arnold Rothstein. He'd been shot and killed after a gambling argument. Arnold figured the poker game he was playing was rigged and once he'd amassed a six-figure debt, he'd asked for some time to pay and at a subsequent meeting, tempers rose until a piece was drawn and fired. Arnold stood no chance and took two days to die. All that agonizing time, he refused to name his assassin to the cops who turned up. He was a stand-up guy to the end.

The four men were all shocked at the news when they heard it, but they understood the world they all lived in.

"We work together, we fight together, but we die alone."

And without Rothstein's ability to find a win-win for all business ventures, cracks began to appear between the various parties who ran chunks of New York, Chicago and the many other cities within Arnold's sphere of influence.

While the four men agreed to eat cheesecake in memory of their dead friend, their need to discuss the state of their precarious empire was pressing on their minds. Meyer spoke for them all when he commented, "Times have been tough without Arnold. He was the ghost in the machine that kept all the parts moving."

"If he was still alive, I would have been able to track down Hayyim."

"Maybe, Alex. But you can be certain that when I find out who put the drop on Arnold, I'll hunt him down and kill him slowly and painfully."

They all knew Charlie meant exactly what he said. He was the closest to the Big Bankroll, and the rumors ran that Arnold had been the first to encourage Charlie into a suit and to dress like a businessman and not a street thug. Hot on his coattails was Meyer who was always smarter than Charlie but lacked the Italian's physical ruthlessness.

Benny's leg constantly twitched as his impatience oozed out of his shaking limb. The man could never sit still, with a constant eye on the next big thing, whether that was a deal in progress or a skirt.

There had been many encroachments on everybody's territories since Arnold's death with no sign of this letting up. Every two or three weeks a hail of bullets and a fresh pile of bodies would head to the morgue.

"The trouble is that the old world order has crumbled away with Arnold's passing and nothing and nobody has taken his place," Alex mused.

"We've got it bad and so has Alfonse."

"What's his problem? I thought he was milking it with booze and gaming."

"Alex, Chicago is still a split town. Alfonse controls the south side but that Irish gonif, Bugs Moran runs the north side."

"Hadn't they worked out a way to keep the peace, Meyer?"

"For a while, they stopped using slugs on each other but there has always been bad blood between them. Now, Alfonse wants to clear the air and put Moran in a body bag."

"Good luck to him, Charlie. From what little I've heard and read in the papers, Moran is no fool."

"You're right, Alex, but Alfonse has a plan up his sleeve and has sought our help."

Meyer and Charlie glanced at each other and then Luciano carried on.

"He asked if you'd be willing to pop over to the Windy City for a day or so."

"Is it necessary? I don't fancy being an assassin for hire, especially for such a high profile hit. Couldn't we send Massimo or Ezra?"

"This needs to be you, Alex. You might not acknowledge it, but you have quite a reputation in the Midwest. Besides, it'll be good for business. Alfonse will owe us a favor and our ties with his Chicago operations will get stronger."

"There's no money in this?"

"I'm sure you can claim your expenses."

Benny spoke for the first time and Alex ignored his sarcastic contribution. This was no laughing matter. Moran was a supremely big fish and his death would have repercussions. That said, Alfonse was doing very well for himself and would be a great partner to have.

"If I get my train fare paid, then I'll do it."

A quick wink in Benny's direction and Alex gouged a huge piece of cheesecake onto his fork and swallowed the large mouthful in one gulp. Benny smiled and his leg stopped twitching for almost five seconds, then resumed its motion.

"That's settled then. When you come back, we'll all be able to enjoy the closer tie with Alfonse. His men are ruthless and have helped us in the past."

"Wire Alfonse that I'll take an evening ride out of town and will see him tonight... Gentlemen, enjoy the rest of your cake, I'm going home to pack."

"Don't spend so long at Ida's that you miss your train."

The three men laughed at Benny's joke.

"No need to worry on that score. She spends too much time with that pipe of hers. Always has."

"You going to replace her with a new model?"

"At some point, Benny. I'm in no rush but I can't see us being together at the end of the year."

With that comment lingering in the air, Alex got up, shook hands with his friends, and headed to Chicago via Ida's bed and his family's apartment.

A CAR MET Alex at the station when he arrived in Chicago and took him to a nondescript hotel. The manager greeted him without introduction and led him to his suite. Ten minutes later, the phone rang and an unknown voice requested his presence in the lobby. Alex agreed and after a short journey, he was sat with Alfonse and several others.

The Italian had chosen a private room at the back of a blind pig in his control. Although it was late, he offered his guests a bite to eat and Alex asked for some sandwiches. The rest of the crew acknowledged they were hungry too and a mound of food was ordered. More predictably, a large round of drinks was requested also, which arrived within minutes.

Alfonse thanked everybody for coming and each man in the room eyed the others up, wondering quite what they were expected to do. Alex recognized only one face: Abe Bernstein, so he knew he was in good company. Next to him was Ron Boaz, a stocky fella with a carefully manicured black beard. There was Fred Burke, thin with wire-rimmed glasses, and a guy introduced as James Morton. Alex got the feeling everyone else knew each other but he couldn't be sure.

"The hit on Bugs Moran will take place tomorrow morning. I would like to thank our friend from the east for joining us. You all know Abe. Thanks for your support in these difficult times. The Sugar House gang has always been a tremendous business partner and I hope our association continues long into the future."

Chicago had been split between Irish and Italian interests since before Prohibition, but the easy money and location of the place conspired to attract the most entrepreneurial fellas from across the region. Alfonse had forged alliances with Detroit and the Lower East Side and Arnold had recognized his talent early in his career.

While Alfonse eyed cute deals, he was prone to erratic outbursts. So when the Irish boss on the north side started to make inroads into Capone's territory, he responded by whacking the guy. That was five years ago and each boss since had died due to excessive quantities of bullets in their brains. No one could say for sure, but word on the street was that Alfonse ordered every hit.

"Abe is supplying the vehicles and other assets for the job but won't be joining you."

"Four of us. How many of them?"

"Can't be precise, Alex. At least five, but there might be ten turn up."

"Those aren't great odds."

"You'll be more than fine. First, you are the most reliable fighters in the country. Second, if your sheer grit isn't enough, I have given you a little edge along the way. Two of you will carry Thompsons."

Alex let out a whistle to show he was impressed. He had used many munitions in his life, but those sub-machine guns had gained a name for themselves in the short time they'd been available on the street. A man could do a lot of damage to another human being with one of those bad boys.

"I'm sure you all have a thousand questions but let me go through the plan before anyone asks me anymore."

Once Alfonse had finished his explanation, he sat down and sipped a whiskey. The others discussed potential weaknesses and Alfonse was open to making any necessary changes. He didn't care about the detail of how Moran died; he just wanted a corpse.

For his part, Alex liked the vision of the plan, but wasn't sure it would work. It was clever—he couldn't deny it—and that was its potential downfall. In Alex's experience, simple always won out over complexity. Given he'd be in the thick of it, he hoped he was wrong. Under normal circumstances, he would have headed straight to the station and back to the safety of New York.

But Alex knew that wasn't an option because they all needed to keep Alfonse happy as there were deals to be done. What worried Alex most was that they had called him in the first place. This was a local problem that could have been handled locally. Alfonse had a reputation himself and Abe and the Sugar House gang were renowned as well.

Had they brought him over from the East Coast to be their fall guy? The idea that he might be their patsy sent a shiver down his spine. If he was right then Meyer, Charlie and Benny had sent him down the river. For the first time since Waxey had plucked him out of the gutter, Alex felt he was closing in on his own death.

38

THE NEXT MORNING a car picked up Alex and brought him to a building near the corner of North Cleveland Avenue and West Grant. They might have been well beyond the safety of Alfonse's reach but there they were inside an office with its windows boarded up, right on the doorstep of Bugs Moran.

Alfonse had supplied a range of firearms for the guys to choose from and two Tommy guns as promised. Alex and Fred were responsible for looking after them and having to take charge of an outfit each. They disrobed and changed into their new clothes while everyone waited. A lifetime later and the phone in the outside corridor burst into life. Fred stood up and hurried to pick up the call. A few words and he hung up on whoever had dropped a dime to this empty building.

"He's been spotted. It's time."

All four strode out onto the street and headed east two blocks until they reached a passageway at the bend of the road which led to North Clark Street. They walked southeast, parallel to the park, and less than five minutes later they halted one hundred feet away from a garage.

As Alex and the crew headed toward the entrance on the other side of the street, he checked up and down the road before he reminded himself of precisely the location of his Tommy inside his long coat and the pistol in his pants pocket. The police uniform felt strange, but he understood that it was an essential but unusual part of Alfonse's plan. No words were spoken, but each man looked at each other for reassurance that all was good. Alex pushed the door open, and they stormed into the garage just as he and Fred whipped out their revolvers and Alex inhaled deeply before he announced their arrival:

"Hands up. This is a raid."

Three guys sat at a table playing cards and four others stood near a vehicle. The hood was up and one of the men wore overalls and had his head stuck into the engine. He was the first to raise his hands and must have been a civilian mechanic. Tough luck on him because he'd chosen the wrong place to work.

Fred headed toward the table and brandished his weapon. Two of the card sharps instantly put their hands on the wooden surface while the one nearest Fred hesitated for a second. Without saying a word, Fred whipped the butt of his pistol sideways, smashing it into the side of the fella's head. The force of the blow caused him to fly off his chair, and he landed on the greasy floor. A woman's revolver lay next to him.

James ran over to pick it up and withdrew a police badge from his inside jacket pocket just before he bent down to collect the piece. The other card players took the hint and dutifully put their hands on their heads. Fred and James continued to train their guns on them.

Meanwhile, Alex and Ron marched over to the truck. By now the mechanic had stepped to one side to separate himself physically from the others.

"We don't need no funny business from you chumps. Put your hands up and face that wall."

Alex's free hand pointed at a long wall at the far end of the garage. It had been painted some time in its life, but you'd be hard pushed to figure out when. The seven men sauntered over, knowing that these cops would frisk them and then seek some financial compensation for not dragging their sorry asses over to the precinct. Police across the country were the same—always after an extra buck and happy to take it from any criminal with the green to supply it.

"Face the wall and assume the position."

Alex's instructions were short and to the point, just like one of Chicago's finest would have said. With Fred and Alex still aiming their pistols at the seven, Ron and James passed down the line to remove any firearms from the assembled throng.

"All clean?" checked Alex.

"As my conscience."

Ron nodded to Alex who glanced at Fred. They took out the Tommys and before any of the Moran crew could respond to the sound of the safeties coming off the submachine guns, Fred and Alex strafed the wall, causing each man's body to drop to the floor within an instant.

A red spray covered the surface and beads of red trickled downward, crisscrossing the rough surface of the paint until it joined the pools of blood pouring out of the corpses. To make sure there were no mistakes, Ron and James fired two shots into each head.

"Time to go. Which one was Moran?"

"Second from the left, I think."

Alex nodded at Fred who smiled back. The smell of death and cordite was in the air, reminding Alex of the trenches. Only for an instant, but long enough for him to want to swallow hard to control his memory of Bobby and the beating of his heart.

"Let's get outta here."

As soon as they got onto the street, they all knew something was wrong. The getaway car was nowhere to be seen.

ALEX'S EYES DARTED around the road again in the hope he'd missed the automobile on this empty scene, but nothing was there. So James and Ron put their hands above their heads while Fred and Alex pointed their revolvers into the small of the civilians' backs. They walked south down the street looking to any casual passerby like two cops taking a pair of felons to the station house.

Sirens wailed in the distance and Fred eyeballed Alex but said nothing. The real flatfeet could be heading straight for them or there could be a bank stickup to attend. No one could tell quite what was happening.

"Where the hell is that car?"

"No idea. Makes me worried we're about to get hung out to dry."

"True, Fred, but Alfonse has always kept his word until now—to me at any rate."

"Same for me, but there's still no getaway in sight."

Two blocks and they carried on walking. There were no cars parked on the street, so no opportunity to boost one and escape. Alex thought he saw the scurrying ants of people five or six hundred feet ahead. They'd need to get off the sidewalk before then.

"Any ideas?"

"Break into an office and lie low?"

"Great short-term solution, Fred. Only problem is that if anyone spots us going in, then we're trapped."

In between the clip-clop of their footsteps came a new sound. It was louder, and therefore nearer, than the sirens but there was nobody on top of them. Alex quickly swiveled around and thought he saw someone vanish into the shadows. He peered into the middle distance but there was no one there, or so he thought.

The four men sped up slightly, all sensing their time would soon be up. The sound of the footsteps behind them increased in volume too. Whoever it was, he was certainly getting closer. Ron was twitchy.

He might have been walking with his hands on his head pretending to be in police custody, but he twisted one way and turned the other as he tried to get a fix on their potential assailant. Then a shot rang out and hell broke loose.

A bullet whizzed past and all four men scattered, each heading in a different direction. The slug had come from behind them and Alex used a trashcan for cover. Fred was on the other sidewalk. Ron and James had lucked out and reached the entrance to an alleyway. This gave them time to yank out their pistols and take aim.

Alex didn't have that luxury, but seeing the general direction of fire, he pulled out his Tommy gun and let a magazine empty into the air. One man collapsed to the floor, twitching.

"How many, Ron?"

"One down. I haven't spotted any others."

"Me neither," added James.

"You reckon it's safe?"

"For now."

They gathered themselves together and dusted their clothes down.

"Should we take a long route round and swing by the safehouse?"

"That was the original arrangement, Alex, but now I'm not so sure."

"We can't stay dressed as cops all day. And you're right, Alfonse's plan bit the dirt the minute some schmendrick forgot to pick us up."

The four men stood at the back of the alley in silence as each weighed up the best way to proceed. Alex was the first to speak.

"You two should get out of town immediately. If you're quick, you might even make it to the train station before the jig is up. Fred, you and I need fresh clothes unless we can steal a car and hightail it out of the city. So I suggest we head over to the safehouse. If we get a vehicle along the way, excellent. If not, we change back into our civvies and blend into the crowd more easily."

"Agreed, but these streets have eyes everywhere. We are deep inside the North Side with no cover. One fella has already found us and who knows how many more will follow."

"And your point is…?"

"Alex, we're dead meat if we stay on the street."

Fred was right. They were sitting ducks on the sidewalks. Then Alex had an idea.

"Good luck, you two. See you soon, I hope."

Handshakes for everyone then Ron and James popped their heads round the alley entrance and Alex heard their footsteps scampering into the distance. Once they were out of sight, Alex turned to Fred and said, "Follow me."

Over to a derelict house on the other end of the alleyway and Alex jumped up and grabbed at the fire escape ladder until he was able to pull it down. They clambered up the side of the building until they reached the top.

From one rooftop to another, the two men sprinted over the blocks out of sight from any nosy civilian who might have wanted to rat them out. The only present danger was leaping from one building to the next, but they were densely packed in this part of town so the jump wasn't too big.

Every so often, the two would drop to the first floor, scurry across a street and then back up to the skyline. Eventually they arrived at the safehouse and waited to check what was happening before they went in. All appeared calm with no one coming or going for a full ten minutes. They took their lives in their hands and hopped inside.

SIX HOURS AND three stolen cars later, Alex and Fred arrived at the outskirts of Detroit. They had taken turns behind the wheel with the other riding shotgun. With Fred at the wheel, they didn't take long to drive over to Abe's headquarters where they were met by Ron and James who'd got in by train some two hours earlier.

"Any word from Alfonse?"

"Yeah, by the time we arrived, he'd already apologized to Abe. The getaway car had a flat."

"You're kidding me."

"Nope, nothing more sinister or complicated than that. That's life."

Abe entered the room and gave Alex and Frank a manly hug each.

"Good to see you both again. Sounds like you had an adventure from what James was saying."

"It had its moments."

"You can tell me over dinner. Please stay here as my guest before you go back east."

"With pleasure. I'll just need to make two phone calls, if I may."

"Of course. You can use my office."

The next morning, February 15, Alex picked up the newspaper which had been delivered to his hotel suite along with his breakfast. As he munched on his toast, the front page was filled with details of the previous day's massacre in a Lincoln Park garage in Chicago. Seven had been slain but Bugs Moran had not been one of the dead.

MARCH 1929

39

DESPITE FAILING TO whack Moran, Alfonse sent word to Alex of how pleased he was with the efforts of the assassination squad. Several of Moran's inner circle were dead and the man himself was scared that Alfonse would make another attempt on his life. While the fella hit the mattresses, Capone took advantage and rampaged through Moran territory.

Alex had lost count of the number of times he had swung by Meyer's office, but now he found himself sat with Charlie, Benny and Lansky in the same comfortable armchair as before.

"Ever since Arnold passed away, God rest his soul, financing our ventures has proved difficult. The stability that Arnold's business relations delivered has floated off too."

"Charlie, you are right. The time we spend chiseling at territory or defending our own turf could be better spent making gelt. We are all losing out."

"While all this chaos is raining down on us here, we should seek fresh opportunities in other parts of the country."

"Benny, you forget we don't have any solid financial backing no more. Breaking new ground costs money."

Benny stared daggers at his old friend and compatriot, Meyer. They had grown up together and, despite some of their differences as adults, they respected each other—even when Meyer started doing business with the Italian, Charlie 'Lucky' Luciano.

"Arnold believed in bringing people closer. We wouldn't know each other if it wasn't for him. Perhaps we should follow his lead."

"Alex, Arnold only worked with men of honor. None of the momzers trying to hem us in can be trusted further than I spit."

Meyer was right. The various gang bosses north and west of their territory couldn't give their word on Monday and still mean it on Tuesday. They would never become partners. Maranzano and his Jewish friend would need to be taken out. The only question was when, not if.

"Meyer, Maranzano knows we do business together, and he tries not to encroach on your operations."

"You are right, Charlie. But don't pretend he shows me the same courtesy. Time and time again, he and his lieutenant have targeted not just me, but my family as well."

"And that was unforgivable. As I told you when that happened, Maranzano claimed he did not authorize that action."

"You believe him?"

"From the expression on his face, yes. But that doesn't mean he did anything to find the culprit either."

"Damn straight."

Just as every other occasion when the kidnapping came up, the men fell silent. While they all believed Maranzano should have routed out Hayyim and punished him appropriately, everyone did business with him and wanted the situation to fade away. Charlie was in a more complex state because Maranzano offered him protection. Charlie worked with Meyer and Arnold despite Maranzano, whose dislike of Jews was well known.

With only the sound of the clock ticking in the background, Alex returned the group from their collective reverie.

"We have men bleeding in the street and liquor being stolen from our warehouses. The cops are standing back to let each of our outfits tear a pound of flesh from the other. What are we going to do about it?"

"Take the fight to them."

"Benny, we've been doing that for months and nothing changes."

"Then we need to be more targeted. Why don't we cut off the head of the snake?"

"Whack Maranzano?"

Charlie looked askance at Benny. The Italian had known his friend from when they ran craps games in short trousers. Maranzano had taken care of Charlie all his adult life and given him power in his organization while he earned vast sums thanks to funding by Arnold. With the Big Bankroll dead, Charlie didn't want to face the prospect of sending his second father to the morgue. Benny continued outlining his logic out loud:

"So, if we don't target the boss then let's figure out which operations or people will cripple him the most and attack them now."

"Without his warehouses, he is nothing. If we squeeze his supply lines, then he'll be on his knees in a flash."

"Meyer is right. A two-pincer movement should do the job. We hit his warehouses and any route into the city that he uses. Until now, we thought scaring his customers away would do the trick."

FIRST, ALEX AND his crew launched a series of attacks on every known storage facility run by Maranzano. Ezra and Massimo made sure that anyone fleeing the scene was gunned down and left to bleed to death on the sidewalk. After two days, Charlie informed the group that Maranzano's speakeasies were running dry and they should expect some mighty retaliation.

Second, Alex asked his out-of-town connections in Windsor, Detroit and Chicago to refuse to do business with Maranzano by promising to buy any goods they usually sold to the Italian on at least the same terms. Abe Bernstein and Alfonse understood what Alex was up to and looked the other way at this Manhattan squabble.

On the third day, Maranzano retaliated. A fire ripped through Alex's office building in what was a clear warning for him to back off. Civilians ran in all directions as the flames tore through each floor. Alex arrived late that morning but Ezra had made a lucky escape.

"The smoke, Alex. It took over the place in just a few minutes. For a second there, I didn't think I'd make it out in one piece. The screaming and shouting. There were women getting trampled in the rush for the exit. I mean, I don't blame anyone for wanting to get out quick, but…"

"…there's no need to kill someone along the way."

"Right."

"Pour yourself a drink and check on your men. If Maranzano has left his mark here, he's no doubt done the same in other parts of the city."

Ezra nodded and walked away to clear his lungs and follow Alex's orders. Massimo arrived on the scene with his jaw at his knees and Alex filled him in on the day's events.

AN HOUR LATER, Alex sat with his two lieutenants in Ida's apartment. There was nothing to link him directly to the residence, and he figured it would be safe for now. On hearing about her visitors, Ida made herself scarce.

"Abe has told me that he won't sell liquor to us for the moment. Seems like Maranzano's guys have attacked every convoy that's left Detroit since yesterday afternoon. Abe's caught between a rock and a hard place. All he wants to do is ship booze out of his town, only his two biggest clients are swinging at each other from beyond the county lines. He can't win."

"Neither can we, Alex. It'll only be a day or so and our blind pigs will be dry. And without a well from which to draw more gin, we lose our customers and they'll move somewhere else."

"Massimo, where do you think they'll go? Off to the Bronx or Queens? I doubt it. No one wants to leave the neighborhood for a brew. It's not losing johns that's the problem; we can't defend every speakeasy, gaming joint and brothel from attack. The cops can see we are on our knees and they appear good to Joe Public by watching us scratch each other's eyes out. What we must do is to avoid hurting any civilians. That never plays well in the papers."

"And when are we going to take out Maranzano? He's the canker."

"That is one mighty powerful man. Before you put a bullet in his brains, you'd better make sure that his business partners are comfortable with your actions. And we've not even started that round of negotiations. He has connections in Sicily and I need not tell you, Massimo, what that means."

Ezra remained unimpressed.

"He's just a man. Any sniper could take him out with a single slug. Nobody would know who had pulled the trigger."

"You understand it's never as simple as that. The killing is the easy part—it's keeping the world from falling apart afterwards that's difficult."

"I guess…"

"Besides," continued Alex, "Charlie tells me that Maranzano's hand is not behind this, anyway. It's Hayyim. Maranzano supports him, but he is the driving force for these attacks. The old Italian has deep pockets and is prepared to wait out the storm. Hayyim is baying for blood, mine in particular."

"Does Charlie know why you're in his crosshairs?"

"Nope, but the guy doesn't just want me dead. He wants me to suffer, my family to suffer and for my business associates to suffer too."

"Nice piece of work."

"He'll get his. That's a stone-cold promise to you. In the meantime, let's figure out how we will make some money tomorrow."

40

FOR THE BRIEFEST of moments, a calm descended on the Lower East Side, which was precisely when Alex got a call from Alfonse who had issues of his own.

"Do you remember my North Side problem you helped me with last month?"

"How could I forget?"

"Well, that itch still needs scratching, and I was wondering if you could visit Chicago and bare your claws."

"We are facing our own problems in New York but things are quiet —for now at least."

"So when can you get over?"

"I'll take the first available train, but I might need to dash back with little notice."

"That's as much as I might ask."

"Just no more dressing up."

The fight with Bugs Moran had continued ever since Alex had fled the Windy City and Alfonse was tired of wasting time on the Irishman.

"We have problems. I need you to show your face and put some fear into those Irish hearts. They've grown so accustomed to my men that those fellas aren't rattled anymore."

"And they should be. You know me, Alfonse, I'm always here for my friends."

ALEX AND CAPONE sat opposite each other at a convenient drinking club deep in the South Side. They'd spent only thirty minutes together since Alex's arrival in town at lunchtime the same day.

"With Moran pushing hard, would you be willing to walk into one of his blind pigs and put on a show?"

"Anything to entertain the troops."

"I'm more interested in scaring his customers and men."

"That's what I meant."

IT TOOK NO time to equip Alex with some firearms and hustle him twenty blocks north, where he and two of Alfonse's guys stood outside the Black Rabbit, looked at each other for less than a second, and walked inside.

They sauntered past the doorman and headed straight for the bar where they ordered a coffee and gin. Drinks served, the fellas wandered round the room until they found an empty table among the crowd. The place was packed—a large open space filled with men and women sitting at tables and chairs barely big enough to sustain their weight.

"This will not be easy."

Alex eyed the location of every fella he could see. His biggest concern was that there were so few guys on the floor. If he was lucky, Moran's gang was cocky and if Alex was not, then the cockroaches would come out of the woodwork as soon as he fired the first shot. The guy remained at the door and there were only two others, one at the far end of the bar and the other positioned on the opposite wall.

"Follow my lead. Let's get this done."

His two new colleagues nodded and gave Alex the space to stand up. He judged the right moment and wended his way over to the counter then moved down as though he was trying to avoid the crowd. Eventually, Alex stood next to the Moran bouncer.

"Got a light, Mac?"

The brown eyes stared at him like he hardly existed. Alex averted his gaze and mumbled something about needing a book of matches. A heavy sigh and a lighter was procured. Then Alex leaned in to enable the end of his cigarette to reach the flickering flame.

Just as the guy fumbled around putting the lighter back into his pocket, Alex pulled out a Barlow knife and plugged the guy in the stomach. A quick twist and he removed the blade then propped up the fella to glide him over to a chair in the corner. The body slumped onto the item of furniture, which enabled Alex to drag the corpse through a nearby door.

Alex held his breath until he found out if his gamble to move a body into an unknown place had paid off. The room was pitch black and Alex scrambled round to find a light switch. When he succeeded, he exhaled and looked around; boxes everywhere, some on the floor, others on shelves.

With one of the three guards taken care of, Alex returned to the main room and his eyes darted around to check everybody's position. Alfonse's men had stationed themselves near the two security guards he'd spotted before. The trouble was that a pair of new fellas had appeared from nowhere—or, more precisely, from a door on the other side of the tables and Alex had no clue how many more were waiting in the wings.

The clock was ticking until the barkeep noticed his watcher was missing, so Alex had little time to think or weigh up his options. He planted both feet firmly on the ground, whipped out a pistol and aimed at the chest of the guy at the door.

A red spray burst out of his back and people began to scream at the sound of the gun and the results of the slug's trajectory. As the other two of Moran's men drew their revolvers, Alfonse's guys had already taken aim and shot at them. Each body flew backwards from the proximity of their assailants. Lots more screaming so Alex fired several bullets into the ceiling.

By now, many people had hit the dirt and were cowering under their tables. Others sat where they were, frozen by fear and indecision. Alex moved around them, continuing to fire into the air, until he reached the entrance. Only then did Alfonse's guys follow him out. As they ran over to him, another fella appeared from the far-side doorway.

"This is it."

Alex aimed and squeezed the trigger. Click. The chamber was empty. He took his second pistol from his other pants pocket, smiled and blasted a hole through the guy's forehead. Alex tutted to himself because he was supposed to get the chest. Either way, the fella was bleeding out on the floor, red seeping through the cracks in the floorboards. No more of Moran's guys showed so the three men turned round and hopped into a waiting car. By the time Alex got back for a drink with Alfonse, a message had been left by Abe Bernstein and Alex was heading to the station and over to Detroit.

"THE COPS CALLED in the Feds and have cut off our liquor supply from Windsor."

Alex's eyes dilated at the news, as he understood why Abe had made him schlep all the way to the dung heap of the world. If he hadn't seen Abe's lips with his own eyes, Alex wouldn't have believed him. The amount of bribe money he'd spent greasing the palms of the local gumshoes over the years would bankrupt an ordinary guy, but Alex was no normal businessman.

He had enjoyed the benefits of being bankrolled by Rothstein, who had advised him to always oil the machine and to keep the little man happy. Arnold might have had huge ideas for the future, but he knew he stood on the shoulders of men who worked harder than he did.

"Why now?"

"You know better than me, from what I hear. Things are hot at home and I had to get you in Chicago. Sounds as though the whole damn country is ready to blow."

"These are nothing more than a few local difficulties. They are just turning up at the same time."

"Keep telling yourself that, Alex. Meanwhile we must secure our boats' safe passage across the Detroit River. We're receiving three big shipments over the next week. If we don't land that hooch then there'll be dry throats coast to coast."

"Find me a long black coat, a fedora and a pair of cop shoes. Time we got closer to the flatfeet, who are kicking at our heels."

Alex grabbed an old jalopy and headed for the river. With no plan in his head, he figured he'd try to sneak near the Feds and see what he could find out. He didn't need to wait too long before he bumped into two guys with cop haircuts under their hats, hanging on a street corner with nothing much to do. One was noticeably taller than the other and Shorty had blond hair.

"Borrow a light?"

Longe Lokshen nodded and passed Alex a book of matches.

"Thanks, Mac. How long you been out here?"

"Since lunchtime, like the rest of the detail. Who are you? Our relief?"

"You're joking. They drafted me in and told me to help, but no one's briefed us properly."

"Ness believes in keeping his cards close to his chest. Doesn't trust anyone."

"We sure live in dangerous times... How long's this operation been running?"

"Three days so far and man it's cold in this city."

Shorty dug his hands deeper into his coat pocket but the wind's chilly bite still cut through him. His companion juddered as a fresh gust sliced through the back of his neck like ice.

"We'd better get used to it. I hear there's another five days of this bull before we have even a chance of going home."

"Yeah, as if we'll walk round the corner and catch the bootleggers red-handed."

Alex enjoyed the irony of his statement. If only these schmucks knew how close they were. Instead, he wished them well and carried on toward the river. The number of times he'd made the crossing meant he knew this part of Detroit like the back of his hand.

Over three blocks to the shoreline and he came across a huddle of men, hiding behind a wall. One was surrounded by the rest and Alex could tell by the body language that this guy was in charge and issuing orders. He sidled up and stood near the back. The inspector was taking questions.

"We have strong intelligence that the Purple Gang are expecting a delivery any day now. We are working with the Mounties on the other side of the river to prevent that from happening."

The Purple Gang was the goyim name for Abe Bernstein's mob and Alex's jaw tightened at the sound of the insult.

"So Mr. Ness we're staying here until the shipment shows?"

"That's the plan, boys."

In that moment, Alex considered following Ness away from this group once they'd finished their pep talk and whacking him. Bury the momzer in the sand by the waterfront.

Then he hatched a simpler plan to send this schmendrick out of town—with a lot less fuss. He vanished into the shadows and returned to his jalopy and drove around until he found a pay phone. Then he dropped a dime.

"Abe, we can get these Feds off our backs before morning."

"How the hell do you propose we do that? You know we don't have the men or the weapons to kill them all?"

"Not one drop of blood needs to be shed."

"I'm listening."

"Send two boats across the river half-full with booze. Make it the good stuff. They are waiting for a massive shipment. If we show them that their rat was only right about the timing but not the quantity, I bet you they'll go home with their tails between their legs. None of the gumshoes on the ground have any appetite to spend the next week standing around the shoreline of Detroit."

"It's worth a try. Who do you think made the call to the Feds?"

"That I don't know, but when I meet the guy..."

41

WHEN ALEX RETURNED home, New York was in turmoil. The number of attacks on his real estate had rocketed in the last day.

"Appears they are hitting us somewhere every hour. It's crazy out there."

"Massimo, do you agree with Ezra?"

A simple nod confirmed Alex's worst fears—just as he was getting someplace in this town and building up proper security, somebody was grabbing at his ankles to drag him back into the gutter.

"Are the cops earning their fees?"

"Not at all. They've turned their backs on us. I tried leaning on them but they don't seem to care. It's like someone has put a fix in with them."

"Ezra, I think I can guess who. The best move right now will be to hit the mattresses. We will always find other venues for our speakeasies and there won't be any liquor hitting the city for at least a week. So let's lie low and wait to see what roaches crawl out from under the floorboards."

Massimo and Ezra agreed with Alex, but their expressions showed that hiding did not sit comfortably with either. He offered them a drink from his desk drawer which they declined. After they had departed, Alex locked up the office and traveled home to spend an evening with the kids before he too checked into a fleapit hotel under a false name.

◆ ◆ ◆

AS EVER, AS soon as Alex stepped into the hallway, his boys appeared as though they'd been waiting all their lives to see him. Sarah held back, leaning on the living room door jamb, to allow sufficient hugs to be extracted from their father. Then she stepped forward, placed a gentle hand on his shoulder and stood on tiptoe to give him a welcoming kiss on the cheek.

He struggled to respond but the boys' excitement overwhelmed him and he moved the herd into the sitting room and had almost succeeded when the housekeeper announced that dinner was served. Sarah hustled the kids to their bathroom for some hand washing and led them over to the dining table.

Alex enjoyed these hours and admitted to himself he'd forgotten how much he enjoyed being with his family. They made him laugh out loud and Sarah made him smile inside when her hair was caught in a certain light. Eventually, all the food was consumed and all the silly jokes had been said.

He helped Sarah bundle the boys into their pajamas, teeth brushing, face washing—including behind the ears—and a hop under the covers in time for their papa to read them a bedtime story. As the kids dropped off to sleep, one after the other, Sarah and Alex returned to the sitting room and shared the couch while they both stared into the flames of the fire.

They said little to each other, choosing to spend their time together offering simple physical companionship. Alex found comfort in feeling the warmth of Sarah's body next to his. With Ida, he knew she only remained interested in him for the gifts he bestowed on her. With Sarah, she only expected him to care of her and the kids. It wasn't that she didn't take great pleasure in the beautiful trinkets and pretty clothes. But, if they weren't there, she wouldn't mind, and that was a big difference between her and Ida.

As the clock on the mantelpiece struck ten, they stood up and headed for bed themselves. Under the sheets, they cuddled more and, despite himself, Alex began to feel a renewed lust for his wife.

He was about to take advantage of these fresh emotions when a hail of bullets erupted through the bedroom.

Driven by pure instinct, Alex rolled over Sarah and thudded to the floor. He grabbed her arm and dragged her down beside him. Slugs whizzed past them for a further twenty seconds and then silence.

"You okay?"

Alex saw Sarah nodding in the gloom.

"Stay here and don't move. Keep your head down in case they start up again."

He shuffled out of the room and rushed to the children. Even though they all had windows facing the same direction, the assailants had only targeted the master bedroom. The boys were whimpering but completely unharmed.

Alex drew a deep breath and tried to calm them down. This had all the trappings of one man: Shmuel Hayyim and he would have to pay for putting his family in danger yet again. This was an outrage. No matter what beef you had with a fella, you always kept it strictly business. And this was personal.

Alex stormed out of the apartment and over to his office where he made some phone calls. Ezra arrived first, but he only lived a block away. Massimo took another fifteen minutes as he had to travel east from Little Italy, Maranzano territory.

"Was it Hayyim or Maranzano who gave the order?"

Massimo looked straight into Alex's eyes, and said the single word... Hayyim.

"He's not been seen near Mulberry for weeks, but tonight he appeared at Tony's, between Broome and Grande. It's family owned and nobody bothers anyone there. Very discreet. As I walked over here, I saw him sat at a window seat."

Either Hayyim was getting careless, or he was setting himself up as bait. Whichever it was, Alex put a hand into the bottom drawer of his desk and pulled out two revolvers.

"What do you want us to do?"

"Massimo, walk back to Hayyim and request a meeting in thirty minutes time. Let him choose the location, only it must be a public place and on neutral turf. We will wait here so you can call me with the address."

His instructions issued, one of his most trusted allies vanished into the night and the other sat down until the phone rang. Alex repeated the location and told Massimo to leave Hayyim as soon as he was able. Then Alex stood up and headed for the door, followed by Ezra.

Hayyim had selected a cafe on Fifth, a block away from Lindy's. As Alex and Ezra approached the Diamond, they surveyed the area. Ezra elbowed Alex who cocked his head in the general direction of two fellas leaning against a wall on the other side of the street to the cafe entrance. They stopped for a second so Alex could light his cigarette from a match in Ezra's cupped hands, which allowed Alex to circle round without drawing too much attention to himself.

"You see any others?"

"Nope, but who knows how many might be at the back of the place."

"Why don't you find out. I'll wait a while to give you a chance to go round the rear and then I shall go in. After that, we do what we need to do to kill Hayyim and get out alive."

AS ALEX STRODE to the Diamond's entrance, the fellas stiffened. Out of the corner of his eye, Alex thought he saw them put their hands in their coat pockets ready to draw their guns. Through the window, he spotted a pair of tables, each with two men sipping coffee. When he walked in, a fella from each table stood up and approached him. While one stared right through him, the other patted him down and found one revolver.

"I'll look after that until you leave."

Alex raised one eyebrow and said nothing. Then the guy led him into the middle of the room by a wall. There was a table set for four but only one man sat alone. He took a swig from a glass of red wine, noticed Alex standing five feet away and beckoned him nearer.

He stood up as Alex stepped forward and held his jacket open to show he wasn't packing any heat. Then both men sat down, opposite each other.

"Shmuel Hayyim, stories of your deeds precede you."

"And the name Alex Cohen carries considerable weight in some parts of this town."

Alex gritted his teeth, wanting to reach out and throttle this *farbissener pisher*. Instead he glanced to the back of the cafe but Ezra was nowhere to be seen. Meanwhile, his two escorts had returned to their seats at the front.

"You caused my wife and children much distress earlier today."

"I wish them no harm. The message I sent was aimed only at you."

"But you caused them upset and the matter will need to be resolved."

"Now is not the time for petty squabbles. You and I have plenty to talk about; we have a long history together."

"Only in a way. You have been chomping at my heels for five years."

"I have been following your career for longer than that, Alex."

"Oh?"

"You don't know who I am, do you?"

"A business partner of Salvatore Maranzano."

"Yes, but you knew my uncle."

"Did I?"

Alex was tiring of this man's arrogance. He was circling around but getting nowhere, although this last statement was intriguing. From the moment Alex had seen Hayyim, he felt as though he had met him before, despite Alex knowing this was impossible. He stared at the guy's face until Alex's jaw dropped and he recognized the family resemblance.

"Sammy Levine."

Those two whispered words, now spoken, provided all the explanation why Shmuel had expended so much energy attempting to bring about his downfall. His mind raced back to the days just before he left for the war and Shmuel completed his thoughts.

"You killed my uncle Sammy, stole his territory then ran away before Waxey Gordon could punish you."

"It wasn't like that. Sammy wasn't innocent. He set me up…"

"I don't wish to hear your excuses. I want reparations."

"Before we get round to discussing how to right the alleged wrongs of the past—and of the present—I need to take a leak."

"Do what you must do."

Alex sauntered as casually as he could to the rear of the cafe and into the john. Just before he opened the door, he looked back and saw one goon rise up and walk toward him. The guy would stand guard while he was inside.

Closing the door behind him, Alex pushed at the three cubicle doors. Two swung open and the third was locked. He pursed his lips and let forth a triple whistle. The occupant responded by opening his door and there sat Ezra proffering a pistol.

"There's three at the front, one outside here and Hayyim on his own."

Alex opened the john door and grabbed the guy still standing on the other side. Before anyone in the cafe could notice, he dragged the fella into the john, one palm over his mouth and the other on his wrist, twisting his arm behind his back.

A crack as Alex broke the bone and Ezra popped out from his hiding place to lend a hand. With a silencer on the barrel of his gun, Ezra shot the man at point blank range in the chest. Red gushed onto the floor but the guy was most definitely dead.

A nod and Alex stepped out of the john and headed beyond Hayyim and straight to the three by the door. Shmuel spoke to him as he walked past, but Alex didn't register what he said. His mind was focused on one thing only.

Twenty feet. Ten feet. Five feet. He pulled out his pistol and sent a bullet flying into each of the men in quick succession. He was so fast and the move so unexpected that not one of them had a chance to even draw his weapon, let alone doing anything else about it.

As soon as the other customers in the joint heard the violent retort of the handgun, bedlam let rip. Women screamed, men hid under tables; some even tried to flee. Alex swiveled round and marched to Hayyim's table. The young upstart hadn't moved an inch, transfixed by surprise. How had Alex smuggled a gun into the joint?

"Sammy and I learned one important lesson from Waxey Gordon. We live together, we fight together but you die alone."

Alex straightened his arm, pulled the trigger and a new hole opened up in the middle of Shmuel Hayyim, nephew of Sammy Levine, the man who had given Alex the education he'd never received in the old country and had betrayed him for a handful of dollars.

Ezra tapped Alex on the shoulder and brought him into the moment. People were fighting to escape from the cafe and the two guys outside had reached the entrance.

Alex followed Ezra out the rear and waited in the back alley for the goons to arrive. In a matter of seconds, both lay dead and Ezra led the way for them both to flee. Within an hour, Alex was lying next to Sarah in their bed although she refused to let him touch her.

MAY 1929

42

THE DEATH OF Hayyim sent shockwaves across the city and, the next day, all hostilities stopped as Maranzano saw no reason to continue Hayyim's fight because there was no money in prolonging everybody's misery. The ceasefire persisted for days then weeks. With supply lines freed up, booze flowed from coast to coast and the various mobs and gangs returned to their daily business routines.

As the months passed, Charlie began to piece together a plan to prevent any future infighting. To seal the deal, he invited everybody to Atlantic City to lay out his stall. To Alex's immense pleasure, he was included on the guest list too.

"Tomorrow will be a big day, Sarah."

They sprawled on the couch in the sitting room. The housekeeper had already put the kids to bed and settled in for an evening's knitting.

"I'm glad you're doing well. Passover was too much. All the shooting—and you spent so much time away from us..."

Sarah's voice trailed off, as though her thoughts continued but she didn't want Alex to hear them. This was usually when he reckoned she imagined him with Ida. Since the business with Hayyim, Alex had hardly seen his mistress. An occasional night here or there but nothing more than that. So Sarah's concern was no longer justified.

"You know I'm leaving town tomorrow. I should be back by the evening, but I can't be sure just yet."

"I was only saying… Do you ever think about the times we spent together when we met?"

Alex inhaled and recalled the scenes of him and Sarah holed up in the whorehouse. He'd paid her ten dollars even though he didn't need to. Then he stopped paying, and that was when you might say they first became a couple.

"Feels like a lifetime ago."

"It was—before you went off to war, and I still owed my debt to Waxey."

"Simpler times… before France."

"It changed you. When you came back, you'd hardened."

Alex stiffened, not because she was right, but because he didn't want to think about what he gave up to be the fella to go to Charlie's business meeting. And he resented her for reminding him of that piece of himself long gone.

That was what she did nowadays; be a constant reminder of who he used to be. He might not be with Ida anymore but he wondered if he should still be married to Sarah.

"War does that to you."

"You must have experienced unimaginable horror over there, but that's not what I meant. You've focused so much on the money, sometimes I think you forget the boys and I exist."

"It was never anything like that."

"Don't be so quick to deny it. I'm not accusing you, just saying."

"Everything I have done has been to put bread on the table for you and the kids. Nothing more."

"Yes, you have been a wonderful provider and I am incredibly grateful for that. But you didn't do all that for us. You did it for yourself and we were lucky recipients of the spoils of your personal war."

Alex ground his molars. Right or wrong, Sarah shouldn't speak to him this way, especially the night before Charlie's meeting.

"You're not sounding grateful. From what I remember, you'd still be in the Oregon if Waxey hadn't paid for you to look after me. I cleared Waxey's debt for you from the money I made on the streets. You weren't no angel."

"Alex, don't twist my words. All I'm saying is that you had your own reasons for doing things and we know each other well enough and have been through so much together that you can be honest with me. It's not what you do for a living that bothers me—I've never judged you, nor could I, given my old profession—it's the lies. When you can't bring yourself to tell me the truth, that's when you hurt me."

He felt the heat in his cheeks and noticed his fingertips were buried in the couch arm. He tried his best not to allow his anger to take over. If it did, he might do something unforgiveable or irreversible. He packed his guns early that day, in his briefcase, which was sitting in the hallway, awaiting his departure. Deep exhalation.

"I hardly see her anymore. Almost never."

"The fact you weren't open with me about that girl... it's not that I wanted you to be with any other woman, but I tried to understand that you needed to do so. It was the lying about it..."

She stood up and floated out of the room leaving Alex alone with his thoughts.

ALEX CLOSED THE apartment door behind him as he left for Atlantic City the following morning. Sarah exhaled deeply, then opened her eyes and jumped out of bed. Two cases full of clothes and she dashed into the boys' rooms to stash their things into bags too.

She rummaged around Alex's study until she found where he'd hidden a stack of green bills, knowing he wouldn't care about the gelt. She phoned for a taxi herself so that the housekeeper would have no clue where they were heading.

The boys got dressed, with a little help from Sarah and she cajoled them out of the apartment as calmly as she could. Although Alex shouldn't get back until tonight or tomorrow, she couldn't face what would happen if she bumped into him on the way out.

Five minutes later, the cab pulled out and headed for the tunnel. She was certain what she would do in the next twenty-four hours after they got to New Jersey but anything after that was a blank sheet of paper.

43

ALEX'S CAR SPED away from the apartment and he reminded Massimo that they had plenty of time and there was no need to rush. Ezra sat in the front too to give Alex extra space to stretch out. Everybody understood the importance of today's meeting.

They headed a few blocks south and, without warning, Alex demanded Massimo pull in, then he jumped out of the car and ducked into an alleyway. Ezra and Massimo looked at each other and shrugged.

"Nerves?"

"Maybe."

They were right and they were wrong. A knot contorted itself inside Alex's stomach but it was nothing to do with anxiety. As he'd stared blankly out of the automobile, he shook himself out of his reverie long enough to recognize where he was when he shouted for them to stop.

He ran into the alley at Norfolk and Broome and stopped at the far end round the corner, hidden from view from the street. A smile and he kneeled down by a wall. Behind boxes and muddy dirt, he used one finger to draw a rectangle around a brick. Barely able to get a purchase on it, he dragged the block out of its position.

Alex shoved his hand into the gaping hole and rummaged around until his fingers found their quarry. He hauled the sack onto the ground with a grin on his face, happy and amazed that his stash had

251

survived untouched for over ten years. No one had spent his savings since Alex banked his money before he skipped off to the Great War.

He stuffed the wad of notes into his jacket pocket and hopped back into the car.

"You all right, boss?"

"Couldn't be better. Let's get out of here."

"Sure thing."

CHARLIE AND A fella called Johnny Torrio had hired a banqueting suite so that workers could join together and hold a union meeting, according to the hotel records. Alex knew Alfonse, Meyer, Benny and, of course, Charlie. As everybody sat down at the boardroom table in the middle of the vast space, Torrio introduced Frank Costello, Joe Adonis, Dutch Schultz, Louis Buchalter, Vincent Mangano and Albert Anastasia.

Each of these men owned and ran territory on the Eastern Seaboard or in Chicago. Who was missing? The Mustache Petes, the old fellas who'd formed the Italian gangs after they sailed over from Sicily.

Alex flanked Charlie and Benny, knowing he was in the company of the most powerful men in America. Before he could reflect on the implications of this thought, Torrio stood up and tapped a spoon against the side of his water glass, clinking his makeshift gavel to get everybody's attention.

"Thank you all for coming here today. I need not remind you of what we have achieved over the past ten or twenty years. We have gone from small town hustlers, with all due respect, to business owners with thousands in our pay and influence. Congratulations to you all."

A polite ripple of applause broke out across the assembled Italians and Jews. They quietened down as Torrio continued.

"But we have reached a junction. Since Arnold Rothstein died, we have been fighting among ourselves so much that the Feds have found enough time to organize an elite squad to break our bootlegging operations. We cannot allow them to succeed and I have a proposal which Charlie Luciano and I have put together."

Alex knew Charlie's idea because they'd talked about it at length since Alex proved himself with Hayyim. Each gang leader would join a single syndicate and there would be no more infighting. Each boss continued to own his existing territory and earned an equal say as a director of the board.

If a situation arose that meant one fella wanted to whack someone in a different crew then he would need permission from whichever boss controlled that gang and its territory. If consent was not granted then the syndicate members would listen to both sides and make a final decision.

The genius of the plan was that if the hit was authorized, then a special outfit would carry out the task. That way, there would be no bad blood between gangs as everyone would have already accepted that the Murder Corporation was untouchable.

After much discussion even Benny Siegel, the group's natural maverick, saw the benefits and agreed to join the syndicate as founder members. The meeting broke up and Alex sidled over to Benny and Meyer while Torrio and Charlie worked the room. Eventually, they reached Alex and took him to one side.

"We want you to consider working with Buchalter and Anastasia to form and operate the Murder Corporation."

Inside, Alex glowed, but he didn't know either of the fellas. Obviously, their reputations preceded them but there was no personal connection with them.

"Can I think it over and tell you in a day or two?"

"Of course. The offer is out there."

Alex's chest puffed up and felt like it was ready to explode. He was on the top of the world.

THE FOLLOWING DAY, Ezra parked outside Alex's apartment block. Both Ezra and Massimo had spent the entire journey excitedly discussing the heady realms their boss had reached. He wished them well and entered the building, heading up to the apartment.

In the elevator, Alex reminded himself of the heights he had achieved and that the security his status would give him meant he could focus on rebuilding bridges with Sarah. His desire to see Ida reduced to an all-time low. Key in the lock and Alex stepped into the hallway. He shut the door and called out to Sarah. "Honey, I'm home. Wait 'till I tell you what's happened. It's all going to be different from now on."

THE END

THANK YOU FOR READING!

Get a free novella

Building a relationship with my readers is the very best thing about writing. I send weekly newsletters with details of new releases, special offers and other bits of news relating to my novels.

And if you sign up to the mailing list I'll send you a copy of the Lagotti Family prequel, The Stickup. Just go to www.leob.ws/signup and we'll take it from there.

Enjoy this book? You can make a difference

Reviews are the most powerful tools in my arsenal when it comes to getting attention for my books. Much as I'd like to, I don't have the financial muscle of a New York publisher. I can't take out full page ads or put posters on the subway. (Not yet, anyway).

But I do have something much more powerful and effective than that, and it's something that those publishers would kill to get their hands on.

A committed and loyal bunch of readers.

Honest reviews of my books help bring them to the attention of other readers.

If you've enjoyed this book I shall be very grateful if you would spend just five minutes leaving a review (it can be as short as you like) on the book's page. You can jump right to the page by clicking www.books2read.com/slugger.

Thank you very much.

Leo

SNEAK PREVIEW

In Book 3, Midtown Huckster…

Claudia wandered off to the kitchenette and busied herself with beans and her percolator. Although she hadn't noticed, Alex stood at the far end of the kitchen leaning against the refrigerator. She swiveled round to get some milk and jumped when she saw how close he was to her.

Despite her concerns, she carried on and waited for the water to boil and then she let the coffee bubble away in the upper chamber of the percolator. Alex remained still for the entire time.

A lifetime later, Claudia poured the steaming brown liquid into two cups and brought them into the living room, where she placed them on a table next to her couch. Alex unbuttoned his jacket and sat down at one end, giving Claudia more than enough space without feeling hemmed in. As a precaution she chose to sit in her armchair instead, a few feet further away.

"Thank you, Claudia."

"You're welcome, but I doubt you have come all this way just for a cup of coffee."

"Correct. Recently you found yourself in a situation and I wanted to make sure my people didn't make you feel the least bit uncomfortable."

"Oh no, not at all. They were very nice about it—suggested I went out to get a drink before any trouble started."

"Good. I'm glad. Sometimes my boys can behave inappropriately and forget how they must be respectful around the delicate, fairer sex."

"There's nothing to worry about on that score, Mr. Cohen."

Alex stirred his coffee and stopped as soon as Claudia mentioned his name. Then he continued and took a sip before speaking again.

"You know who I am."

"I didn't recognize you, if that's what you were thinking. One of your guys used your name and I put two and two together."

"You're a bright girl, Claudia. Have you been back to the office at all?"

"I figured you told me to scram, so I did just that. Yesterday evening's paper told me all I needed to know."

"Did they say who did for Maranzano?"

"No, only that it was gang related."

"And what do you think happened?"

"Mr. Cohen, Salvatore paid me to do what he asked, not to think."

"Call me Alex. How well did you know Salvatore?

Claudia blushed and her eyes cast down onto her lap—the rumors were true and that she was one of his many conquests.

"My apologies, it was wrong of me to ask you such a question. Can you forgive me?"

"Of course... Alex."

"Perhaps you'd be interested in carrying on a bedroom arrangement with me instead of Salvatore. You're a fine looking woman, after all."

Claudia's eyes flicked from left to right. She couldn't believe what Alex was suggesting, but it would explain why the gentleman had come calling.

"Well, a girl does have to earn a living..."

"Why don't we start our new relationship now? Hop into bed and I'll be with you in a minute—I need to freshen up first. I hope you don't mind."

"Not at all. It's pleasant having a man around who cares about such things."

She showed him the way to the bathroom and once she'd headed to the bedroom and he could see she was beginning to undress, he popped inside and waited a count of sixty. Then he flushed the toilet, put his hand in his inside jacket pocket and strode into the bedroom.

Claudia lay under the blankets with her clothes strewn around the room. She smiled coquettishly at him and Alex returned her grin. He pulled out his pistol and shot her in the head. Once where he stood and the second time, he stuffed a pillow over her face and squeezed the trigger. Then he threw ten dollars on her bedside table and walked out.

To grab your copy, go to www.leob.ws/huckster.

OTHER BOOKS BY THE AUTHOR

Alex Cohen

The Bowery Slugger (Book 1)
East Side Hustler (Book 2)
Midtown Huckster (Book 3–Out July 2020)
Alex Cohen Books 1-3 (Due Late 2020)
Casino Chiseler (Book 4–Due Late 2020)

Stand Alone

The Case
The Death and Life of Penny Pitstop

The Lagotti Family

The Heist (Book 1)
The Getaway (Book 2)
Powder (Book 3)
Mama's Gone (Book 4)
The Lagotti Family Complete Collection (Books 1-4)

All books are available from www.leob.ws and all major eBook and paperback sales platforms.

ABOUT THE AUTHOR

Leopold Borstinski is an independent author whose past careers have included financial journalism, business management of financial software companies, consulting and product sales and marketing, as well as teaching.

There is nothing he likes better so he does as much nothing as he possibly can. He has travelled extensively in Europe and the US and has visited Asia on several occasions. Leopold holds a Philosophy degree and tries not to drop it too often.

He lives near London and is married with one wife, one child and no pets.

Find out more at LeopoldBorstinski.com.

Made in the USA
Las Vegas, NV
28 October 2021

33249628R00152